THE FAMILY SECRET
A completely gripping psychological thriller
full of incredible twists
Mikayla Davids

For the brilliant book bloggers who support authors, share stories and help to make dreams come true.

Prologue

Silence.

All I can hear is silence.

The world around me is hazy. Crisp, fresh snow, several inches deep, crunches under my heavy boots. The icy caps of the mountain peaks tower above me, appearing monochrome and chilling in the dim light. I inhale the cold air in short, sharp breaths as my eyes adjust to the gloom. The darkness of the night is only just beginning to lift and the sun is still yet to rise.

It's a long time since I've been up this early. And it's eerie, standing here by myself in the middle of this exclusive ski resort without a soul nearby. I'm used to seeing this scene brimming with people in colourful outfits, laughter and chatter swirling in the air around me. But not even the chalet girls are up.

Something jerked me awake from my warm bed, after a brief and fitful sleep. Only a few short hours ago, I was trudging up the hill to my family's holiday chalet, alcohol dulling my senses and urging me forward to the warmth of the luxury accommodation. I couldn't rest properly though, there was something on my mind, something that just didn't feel right.

I retrace the steps I'd trodden only hours before, making my way slowly down the slippery path. My mouth is dry and my whole body feels sluggish, but I keep going. I need to fill in the missing puzzle pieces of my memories from last night. As I slip and slide down the hillside, snapshots of the evening flicker in my mind...

I reach the large chalet and see there's a gap around the door, it's not fully shut. A shiver runs through me. It must be freezing in there. Stepping inside, I survey the scene. The wreckage of the night before is plain to see. Wine bottles clutter every surface, a chair is upturned and clothes are strewn everywhere. But there's no one here. There's nothing but silence. Everyone is long gone.

I'm turning to go, feeling foolish for coming back, when I see something out of the corner of my eye, snagging my attention. I turn fully towards the heap of material in the centre of the room.

And that's when I realise... it's not just a jumble of clothing, there's a person lying there. I see who it is and I start to smile. I should've guessed who would be passed out in the middle of the floor after the heavy night we had.

I call out their name. There's no response so I drop to my knees and brush the hair off their face.

My jaw drops in shock.

This person is too cold, too pale, too lifeless.

The door is still open and a cold blast of wind sweeps into the room, causing snowflakes to flutter into the chalet. I feel numb. This can't be real.

I look back down and that's when I see it.

The knife. And the blood.

My worst fears are confirmed and I spring back with a cry. Panic grips me. I can't be found here.

I rush outside, my heart hammering wildly and my breath catching in my chest as I push myself back up the hillside. One thought circling in my mind:

What really happened last night?

Chapter One

Nadia

To anyone watching, I'm sure we look like a nice, ordinary family arriving for a winter holiday. A woman with her three grown-up daughters and a trio of sleepy-eyed grandchildren. But as soon as anyone learns our names that illusion is shattered.

Because we're the Bailey family.

Our story has been discussed up and down the country, printed in thousands of newspapers and used as clickbait on even more websites over the last month. The media has reported in meticulous detail the events of the lavish Christmas party that was held in a stunning mansion in the English countryside — and the shocking murder that occurred as the clock struck midnight. I've heard the whispers when I've gone to grab milk and bread from our local corner shop in recent weeks and I could see the morbid curiosity in the eyes of the man at the airport check-in desk as he stamped our passports before we boarded the plane to France.

I'm hoping we can leave all that stress behind us and disappear amongst the tourists and the sports enthusiasts during our stay at the stunning ski resort in the French Alps where my daughter Erin owns a chalet. I run my hand through my spiky, blonde hair and then pull my white knitted hat down over my head as I exit the taxi that has dropped us off at the entrance to the resort. A rush of cold air blasts me in the face and steams up my glasses, causing me to blink rapidly. As my vision demists, I take in the imposing outlines of the mountainscape. A full moon hangs in the sky, casting a light across the snow-covered ice caps and enabling me to make out the shapes of the resort's chalets.

I'm over-awed as I drink in the jagged mountain edges and the small smudge of purple colour on the horizon, the last traces of the daylight gradually being swallowed up by the inky night sky. The scenery is even more majestic than I imagined it would be. And yet, for all its beauty, there's a sense of danger and foreboding. The wooden chalets that we pass by are just small specks in comparison to the giants of nature surrounding the man-made ski resort. Goosebumps prickle my skin as I follow my middle daughter who's guiding us closer to the chalet that belongs to her.

Booking this trip felt like the right thing to do – a change of scenery and a chance to get away from the journalists turning up on our doorstep and the questioning eyes of our neighbours. But the journey has been long due to a delay in the plane setting off and we experienced some rough turbulence in the skies. Everyone's patience is now frayed and we're arriving much later than we planned. The freezing cold weather and the downturned lips on my grandchildren's faces make me question if travelling this week was wise. After all, we've just buried a family member and emotions are running high.

The wind whips up around us and I pull my youngest granddaughter close to my side, feeling her quivering against me as the cold seeps into her bones.

There's been too much heartache and too many family secrets in the last ten years. These past few weeks, I've been over and over the events in my mind. I keep waking up in the dead of the night wondering where I went wrong, wondering if it's my fault that my three girls – all grown women in their thirties now – are having such a turbulent time.

I can't decide who I'm most worried about. My eldest Sasha, her dark, curly hair spilling down her back, has a blank expression on her face and my middle daughter Erin's glossy copper-coloured ponytail gleams every time it catches the light but she's walking with an unnatural, rigid posture like she's trying too hard to keep herself upright. Leah, the youngest of the three, has her eyes fixed to the mobile phone clamped in her hand, the glowing screen stealing her attention.

They all have their issues; doesn't everybody? But our lives are unravelling because of that doomed festive party – secrets, lies, revenge and murder... everything imploded at once. Can we move on from it? Can we learn to love and trust each other again?

We're about to find out.

I look around at the spectacular scenery I'm now part of and I pray we've made the right decision to come here.

Chapter Two

Leah

I gasp in surprise as I take in the scene in front of me: it's a perfect winter wonderland. Twinkling lights shine in the darkness, there's a warm glow emitting from each of the many cosy chalets sprinkled across the mountainside and the blanket of snow adds to the fairytale feel of this luxury ski resort. I needed a proper break and this is exactly the escape from reality I had in mind.

Dragging my heavy and slightly battered suitcase behind me, my fingers start to throb a little from the biting cold. I'm just beginning to wonder how much further our own accommodation is when we come to a halt in front of one of the largest and most impressive chalets I've seen so far. My eyes roam over the exterior, there's a bright blue door and enough windows to suggest that the interior of this place is going to be huge.

'Erin, this is incredible!' I breathe.

My sister gives a small smile as she opens the door to her expensive holiday home. 'Step this way, everyone,' she says in a tinkling voice, clearly enjoying playing hostess. 'Welcome to Snowfall Chalet.'

I follow Erin inside and give a little squeak of delight when she taps the electronic control pad and all the lights immediately blink on to reveal the sumptuous alpine interior. Discarding my suitcase in the hallway, I go through to the first room and find an expansive open-plan kitchen and living room. I'm drawn to the far end of the space where there are floor-to-ceiling windows with a stunning view across the resort.

Everyone else files into the room. There's my eldest sister Sasha and her daughter Freya; my mom, Nadia; and my other sister Erin's nine-year-old twins Jasper and Ophelia. We're all in different stages of travel weariness. Arriving at the resort has perked me up and my sister Erin also looks bright-eyed. But my niece Ophelia and my nephew Jasper are sleepy and ready for their beds. They're used to coming here in the winter months so the surroundings aren't a novelty for them.

'Wow!' Freya bounds up to me, echoing my thoughts exactly. 'This is like being in a movie!' She claps her hands together with enthusiasm. For Freya this trip is a big deal. She's the same age as Erin's children but she's never been out of the UK before. Freya is buzzing with excitement; she's twirling around in the middle of the room and her cheeks are flushed.

I hug her to my side and we stand together looking out at the incredible scenery in front of us. I cross my fingers and hope the next few weeks are stress-free for us all. Our family has had far too much drama to deal with recently.

'Calm down a little,' Sasha says with a sigh to her daughter. 'It's been a long journey and you need to get some rest soon.'

Sasha looks absolutely exhausted. She has dark circles under her red-rimmed eyes. She's been through a hell of a lot in the last month. Discovering her husband Jesse had fallen out of love with her and betrayed her in the worst possible way was enough of a punch in the gut, but Jesse's actions then led to the devastating events at Erin's annual Christmas party. It was meant to be an evening for the rest of us to reunite with Erin and reconcile our difference after ten years apart. But what should have been a happy occasion came to an abrupt end. We're all still coming to terms with what happened. So now my mom, sisters and their children are gathered together for a few weeks to heal from the emotional time we've all had and to reconnect with each other.

My mom, Nadia, is the last to filter into the room. She's the matriarch and the person who got us all organised in order to make this family trip go ahead. In her mid-sixties, she looks young for her age, with her short, blonde spiky hair and on-trend clothes. But recent events have taken their toll on her and I can tell by her pinched lips that she feels there's a lot riding on this trip. It's make or break for our relationships and she knows it.

'Oh, Erin, this is just charming.' Nadia admires the alpine chic of the decor. 'Did you design all of this yourself?'

Erin nods in response. I'm not in the least surprised, Erin has always had a creative flair. Of course she did the interior design on this place; I imagine it was a breeze in comparison to the refurbishment of Burcott House, the old English country mansion that she transformed into a five-star hotel. Burcott House, with its lavender fields and lofty ceilings, had been owned by her husband's family for generations. It had been falling into disrepair until Erin breathed life back into the property and revamped it as a boutique hotel and upmarket wedding venue. The same can't be said of her husband Aaron himself. He took his last breath at the hotel a little under a month ago. His death was not peaceful or expected.

He was murdered.

Aaron died after plunging from a twisting staircase onto the cold, unforgiving marble floor below.

We've all been reeling ever since. Even though my history with Erin is complicated, I've done my best to rally round, to help out with her kids. Because I know what it's like to lose your father at a young age, so I've wanted to be there for Ophelia and Jasper and to support them through this difficult period. Things have been even tougher because of who murdered Aaron.

It was Sasha's husband Jesse.

None of us can quite believe that Jesse is a killer. He's been part of our family for so long and he's like an older brother to me. He's the last person in the world I would have felt unsafe with, but I was there when he confessed to the crime. In a moment of madness he snapped in an argument with Aaron and threw him over the bannister to his death.

Now nothing will ever be the same again.

Ever since that night, Sasha has been like a zombie, just going through the motions of day-to-day life but not really living it. I brush a stray strand of my light blonde hair behind my ear and turn my attention to the children. 'Bedtime then.' I smile at all three of them. 'Ophelia and Jasper, can you show us where you'll be sleeping?'

The three kids stream out of the room in front of me and Sasha shoots me a grateful look. Her curly, dark hair is frizzy from the light drizzle of snow earlier. She slumps down onto the sofa, a frown line imprinted on her forehead. I'm worried about her and I'm hoping this break away will give her time to relax and rest. Getting the little ones into bed is just a small thing but I'm happy to play the doting auntie and take the pressure off my two sisters. I have no offspring of my own and spending time with my nieces and nephew is about as close as I intend to get to parental responsibilities at this stage in my life. I'm currently very happy with being fun Auntie Leah.

The next half an hour is a whirl of finding toothbrushes, washing faces, hurried bedtime stories and tucking three little bodies into fresh bedsheets.

'Goodnight,' I say softly as I click off the light in the room the three of them are sharing. They all look worn out enough that I'm sure they'll drop off quite quickly.

I re-enter the central room in the chalet to find a fire crackling in the grate and my mom and two sisters circled around it in various comfortable chairs. My mom has a blanket draped over her and I squidge in beside her and pull some of of the soft fabric over my lap.

'Thanks for that Leah,' Sasha says drowsily. She's still on the sofa, her legs now up on the footstool. She looks as though she's been dozing. Erin is still scrolling on her iPad, completely engrossed, and doesn't look up.

'Well, isn't this exciting!' Mom says, in a light-hearted tone that sounds too forced to me.

Sasha and Erin briefly catch each other's eyes and a look of under-standing passes between them. They've both had their hearts ripped out as a result of that disastrous Christmas party so 'exciting' doesn't quite reflect their state of play currently. However, this brief interac-tion is the first time I've seen the two of them show anything close to kinship for a very long while, so I cross my fingers under the blanket. This break might just be the fresh chapter we all need to move forward.

'What time are the skiing lessons tomorrow, Erin?' Mom quizzes. 'Nine-thirty for the children and ten o'clock for you three'. Erin is a proficient skier so doesn't need lessons like the rest of us but Mom and Sasha have mostly skied on dry slopes or artificial snow. I've never skied at all before but I'm looking forward to learning. We're planning to make the most of the experts out here and Erin has advised us that, in this setting, we can all get up to a passable level quickly.

'Leah, I hear that Xavier Knight is out here at the moment as well,' Erin says.

'Really?' I try to keep my voice casual but the truth is I get butterflies when Erin tells me this.

'Yes, really.' Erin gives me a little smirk.

I met Xavier at Erin's Christmas party and was instantly attracted to him. He's a family friend of Erin's and he told me he was planning to be skiing in France for the early part of the year. With everything going on after Aaron's death, I've only exchanged messages and seen him briefly once since the party. But the idea of a serendipitous meeting with the tall and attractive Xavier sets my heart beating a little faster. He's single, wealthy and likes to travel. Xavier is the first guy in ages who seems to have everything I've been looking for in a partner.

I twirl a lock of hair between my fingers. Perhaps for once I might be lucky in love, because I've made too many mistakes on the dating front in recent years. My last, messy relationship has been by far the most awful. I'm determined to finally shake myself free from that entanglement once and for all. A winter romance in this scenic part of the world could be just the thing to help me move on.

We all lapse into silence once more. My mom is flicking through an old paperback, Erin's attention is back on her iPad and Sasha is gently snoring. So I don't feel bad about pulling out my phone and going through my notifications and emails. In my line of work as a social media influencer keeping up to date with everything sometimes feels impossible. I've been trying to set myself better habits with my social media interaction but I can't seem to prevent myself from a late-night check through everything before bed. It's almost as though I have to tidy away my online persona for the day before I can even think about resting myself.

I've just finished pinging off a few quick email responses to my manager when a message pops up on my screen. It's from an unknown number and immediately my stomach turns to ice.

I click into the notification and my anxiety instantly ramps up as I scan the content.

I'M AT THE SKI RESORT.

Biting my tongue, I try to tell myself the message could be from Xavier – he might have texted from a different number to the one he originally gave me and Erin has literally just said he's staying at this ski resort. Except my instinct is telling me this communication is very much not from him. For starters his style is different and he usually signs off with a multitude of kisses.

This was meant to scare me. And it has.

I've had enough creepy contact from stalkers and keyboard warriors over the years I've been building my social media brand. But, in the last few months, things have escalated a lot. One person has been relentless in their cyber threats and blackmailing. The activity had eased off in the last few weeks and I'd thought they'd got fed up and might start to leave me alone.

No such luck.

If it's the same person, they've been lulling me into a false sense of security. Another possibility is that someone's figured out my connection to Erin and Sasha. Their names have been splashed across news stories about Aaron's death. It's only a matter of time until my followers connect the dots and realise I'm the third Bailey sister. Now I feel queasy at the thought that I'm going to be confronted by some crazed stalker on the slopes. It's as if the Bailey family is cursed.

I should go straight to the police and report this but it's a little more complicated than that. So I've just got to hope this is an empty threat and whoever is behind it isn't going to materialise in real life.

I aimlessly flick through my phone, not really paying any attention to the endless footage of cats doing ridiculous things and inspirational life quotes flooding my social media algorithms. My mind is now racing with thoughts – is the person behind the message the same person who's been stalking me? How did they know I was here? Is this somehow connected with Aaron's death?

And how afraid should I be?

Chapter Three
Nadia

I swirl the spoon around in the mug and inhale the delicious, sweet smell. Steaming hot chocolate with a tot of bourbon felt like the best way to round off our long day of travelling. I take a handful of mini marshmallows and sprinkle them over the top of the four drinks. My girls may now be adults but they all liked mini marshmallows and hot chocolate when they were little. And favourite childhood treats are often the best kind of comfort as an adult.

Sometimes I long to have those early years back again. I was sleep-deprived for sure, and the days used to rush by in a blur of mealtimes, scraped knees and cuddles but they were simpler times too. I've found being a parent to grown-up daughters a lot more challenging than the days of school pick-ups and teddy bears' picnics. And the last month has tested me to my absolute limit.

'Here you go,' I say to my youngest daughter Leah, passing her mug to her.

'Ah, thanks Mom. This looks divine.'

I smile at her use of 'Mom'. Leah, trying to make herself stand out against two older sisters, decided as a teenager to call me Mom instead of Mum like the other two. This was also partly down to our mutual obsession with American sitcoms, *The Gilmore Girls* being our favourite. Leah has continued to make herself stand out ever since and she's built a successful career as an influencer as a result. I don't really understand all the details of what she does, but she's jetting around the world and making decent money. And I couldn't be prouder of her for following her dreams.

Leah settles back into her seat, her attention pulled straight back to her phone. She absent-mindedly runs a finger over the scar on her temple. It's faded so much over time and Leah usually covers it up with make-up, but it's still there. It's an ever-present reminder of the night ten years ago that first splintered our little family. Leah was run over on a dark country lane.

By Erin.

Erin and I had just had a huge argument. I can remember the events as vividly as if they were yesterday. She shouldn't have got into the car but I let her go. I will always feel responsible about that.

Gazing at my three grown-up daughters, flashbacks play out in my mind. Erin screeched off into the pitch-black night and the accident which followed put Leah in hospital for months. The subsequent argument tore my family apart. Sasha was furious with Erin and Leah couldn't immediately forgive her. I should've realised it was going to take time to get over what happened. None of us dealt with the situation well. It resulted in Erin not speaking to us for a decade while Leah went travelling to far-flung corners of the Earth as soon as she was recovered, leaving me with just Sasha by my side.

I place a drink in front of Erin and she gives me an appreciative nod. My middle daughter is a precious sight to me. In the years we were estranged, I dreamed of seeing her pretty heart-shaped face every single day. When the initial anger from Sasha and Leah had fizzled out and they were ready to forgive her, Erin no longer wanted anything to do with any of us. I tried and tried to talk to her but Erin is stubborn and she kept pushing me away. So when I received her invitation to her annual Christmas party last month I was over the moon with joy. A decade of sadness was coming to a close... or so I thought.

I sigh. Tugging my gaze away from Erin auburn hair I move to pull off my jumper, suddenly feeling restricted by the heavy material. It should've been a wonderful evening for a family reunion. I finally had all three daughters together after ten years. And it was the perfect time of year for forgiveness, except Aaron's untimely demise shattered the celebrations. I think we're all still in a state of disbelief. If I close my eyes, I can still see his broken body splayed out on the white marble floor. I wasn't sure if my family would weather the events of that night. The tentative new relationship with Erin was still only hours old but, instead of shutting me out, she's let me help her through the last painful few weeks. I've spent time with her and her twins and, even though the circumstances have been tough, I'm determined to be there for them and to make up for all that missed time.

Surprisingly, Erin has let her sisters in as well. Given that Sasha's husband Jesse was responsible for Aaron's death, I was afraid it would deepen the rift between my daughters. But instead it's had the opposite effect. They've not talked things out yet but they've tolerated each other and, in my book, that's a massive improvement on not speaking at all. The fact they've been in each other's orbit is a step forward in the right direction and I hope that one day they will become friends as well as sisters.

I go back to the kitchen, with its high-end appliances and ultra-modern design. Erin organised for the cupboards to be fully stocked ahead of our arrival. It baffles me that in a place like this you can pay for someone to do your shopping and pack it away onto the correct shelves. It's a far cry from the life I was living as a young single mother to three children. If you'd told me back then that Erin would grow up to be a millionaire, I would have had a hard time believing a girl who was raised on a council estate would ever have the opportunity to rise so high. This really is Erin's world now though. She was rich by association because of her marriage to Aaron and she's rich in her own right since her husband passed away, leaving all his wealth and assets to Erin and the twins.

Plucking the two remaining mugs from the countertop, I hand one to Sasha and then plonk myself back down in my own seat. The fire is emitting a pleasant warmth and I feel grateful to have my girls under one roof, with the children sleeping soundly in their beds.

'Ouch!' Sasha exclaims. 'That scalded my tongue!'

'Sorry love, it was fresh from the hob.'

Sasha pulls a face of annoyance and then pads over to the kitchen. I hear the tap go on and assume she's splashing some cold water in her drink to cool it down. I get the feeling she's probably ready to go to bed by this point. When I don't hear her padding back towards us, I twist slightly in my seat and notice Sasha pouring another generous measure of bourbon into her mug.

I turn around again before she catches me looking at her, but I'm not happy about what I've just witnessed. Sasha has been drinking a lot over the last few weeks. She may think I haven't clocked it, but I saw her recycling bin stuffed full of wine bottles before we left home for this trip. I'm worried about her. At first, I tried to pass her drinking off as her taking advantage of the festive period and as her knee-jerk coping mechanism following the revelations about Jesse that led to him being arrested and to their marriage ending. I can't quite imagine how she felt, having her world implode in one evening. But as the weeks roll on, I'm getting concerned that she's drinking herself into a rut that she won't be able to get out of easily. We're at the end of January now and she's showing no signs of stopping so I know that very soon I'm going to need to step in and intervene.

'Night all,' Sasha calls, and then slinks off to the room she'll be sharing with me. The two of us are in single beds in the smallest room, although even the smallest room is very well proportioned. Next to our bedroom is the children's, complete with two sets of bunk beds. Erin and Leah both have rooms with king-sized beds. I had hoped that Leah might offer the king-size bed to Sasha, given the circumstances, but Leah seemed keen to hold onto a room with an ensuite. I guess it means she has the space to spend on her make-up, which is important to her because of all the filming she does for social media videos.

Leah is frowning at her phone right now, her blue eyes captivated by the content she's scrolling through. Her neck is bent at an unnatural angle and I want to tell her to sit up straight, otherwise she'll have posture issues before too long. I hold my tongue though; me nagging is the last thing any of these girls need. Leah's posture will have to wait; it's their happiness and mental wellbeing that I need to work on first.

'Right, I'm going to turn in now as well,' I announce after I've drained my hot drink. I stand up and drop a kiss on Leah's head and go to do the same to Erin. She stretches backwards away from me though and offers a perfunctory 'Goodnight' instead. I give her a meaningful smile and try to communicate that I love her with the look in my eyes instead. It's still early days for Erin and I, so I don't want to push things too far and risk losing her again.

I would do anything for my children and grandchildren. They mean the world to me. I just wish I could shield them from all the bad things – and people – in this life. That's unrealistic though and, if there's anything I've learnt on my journey of motherhood, it's that you must teach your offspring survival skills. Wrapping them in cotton wool ultimately isn't going to protect them – it might do more damage than good, so arming them with the skills to look after themselves has always been my number one priority. To some extent, it's paid off. All three of them are warriors – women who on paper have a string of incredible achievements between them. Sasha is an assistant headteacher, Erin runs her affluent hotel and wedding business, and Leah is adored by her millions of followers across the globe. They've all achieved success in different ways but the element of their lives that all three of them have experienced struggles in is their love life. And I wonder if they've inherited that attribute from me...

I head to the shared bathroom and drag a brush through my short hair. Surveying the face in the mirror, I still can't get used to this older version of myself – I always expect thirty-year-old me to be in the reflection. Using a reusable cleansing cloth, I quickly wash away the remnants of my foundation and blusher. A few more worry lines and wrinkles have been added to my face recently but with everything that's been going on I'm not exactly surprised.

Tiptoeing into the room I'm sharing with Sasha; I silently slide into bed and take a second to appreciate the high-quality silk sheets. I'm not used to the kind of lifestyle my daughters have crafted at all. I still save the change from my pint of milk and buy most of my things second-hand. Old habits die hard. I allow my mind to relax and tune into the steady rhythm of Sasha's breathing as she sleeps.

I'm aware that I've got my work cut out, not just in the next few weeks, but for a good while yet if I'm going to get anywhere near close to the happy family scenario that I'm striving for. It will be hard, and I'm sure there'll be plenty of tears along the way, but I'm determined to strengthen our unit. To get to a place where my daughters trust each other again. At least we don't have the added complexity of any of us having partners in the mix. I haven't had a serious relationship since Simon, the love of my life and Leah's father, died unexpectedly many years ago when my children were still little. Erin is now a widow; Sasha's husband is in jail and Leah hasn't shown any interest in settling down at all. It seems the Bailey women are destined to be forever unlucky in love. At least it means we can focus on ourselves for the time being and I'm thankful about that. After all, Jesse is at the heart of our family's issues. If he hadn't come along maybe things would've turned out very differently for all of us.

As I'm drifting off, I think I hear someone crying. It's not Sasha, as she's only metres away from me. Leah's room is at the other end of the hallway and the children's room is next to hers. But the sound isn't coming from that direction, which means it must be Erin in the lounge. Erin is the least likely of my three girls to cry. Even as a child, she had a steely exterior about her and she rarely displayed outbursts of tears. It must be her though. She wouldn't appreciate me intruding right now if she's upset, so I make a mental note to try and get some alone time with her soon. Her husband's murder is affecting her and she needs to open up about it and get everything off her chest. There are things Erin and I need to talk about.

It's up to me to be strong for my daughters. I'm going to do whatever is needed to steer them through this rough patch and towards happier waters.

I've already lied to the police in order to keep one of them safe.

And I'd do it again if I had to.

Chapter Four

Erin

I'm so relieved to be away from Burcott House and the pressure of pretending to be the grieving widow. I twist my gold wedding band on my finger, nestled next to my huge rock of an engagement ring. I've kept both rings firmly in place, as an outward show of my devotion to my recently deceased husband. Inwardly, I'm wondering when I can sell off the jewellery and exactly how much my engagement ring will fetch. I'm planning to treat myself to a new ruby-studded band, to symbolise the start of a new chapter in my life. This time, I'm in control of what happens next. I don't have my bully of a husband to answer to any longer. I'm going to make the most of the freedom I've worked so hard for.

I wipe the tears from my eyes, it's been such a nerve-wracking month and sometimes the magnitude of it all is overwhelming. I'm not usually an emotional person but everyone has their vulnerable moments. Even me.

I stayed at home with Ophelia and Jasper, dressed appropriately in black every day, until Aaron's funeral. It was a freezing cold January morning and it also felt like the longest day of my life. I'm thankful it's all over now. I waited a few days for appearances' sake and then my mother helped me organise everything to ensure all of the Bailey family were on a plane to France by the end of the month. Now we're here, I can relax a bit more. The main charade is done with; I got through it, I fooled everyone.

It was my idea to kill Aaron.

I wanted him out of my life so that I could be free. He was the kind of controlling bully that would never have let me divorce him and move on. He would've ruined me financially and tried to take the twins from me. I wasn't prepared to risk losing everything – my children, my home, my business. If I'd tried to leave he would have used the best lawyers against me. It was extreme but I felt like it was my only way out. It took me several years to work up the courage to take action.

Staring out the window at the snowy mountains, I think about how much has happened since I was last at Snowfall Chalet. Last year, I reignited my affair with Jesse — my sister Sasha's husband. We originally fell in love over ten years ago but the timing was terrible as Jesse was dating Sasha. Jesse was going to leave my sister but then discovered she was pregnant and my mother persuaded him into staying with Sasha. I was devastated. Jesse is the only man I've really loved but he walked away from me.

Another wave of emotion comes over me. Seeing Jesse again hurt like hell but also confirmed he'd regretted his decision and wanted to do whatever he could to show how sorry he was. I told him all about Aaron's behaviour and planted the idea of getting rid of my husband into Jesse's head. We didn't exactly plan for Aaron to die in such a dramatic way. But I can remember the moment when Jesse clapped eyes on Aaron. He hated him at first sight and Jesse's actions were, in the end, fuelled by passion for me. It would have been easy to panic when Jesse shoved Aaron from the twisting staircase but I kept my cool and coached Jesse through the whole thing.

I stand up and pace around the room. Everyone else has gone to bed and I should really do the same but my mind is racing too much. I need to have a few moments of quiet to reflect on everything before I turn in for the night. An email pings on my iPad and automatically I go to check it. It's from my father, Craig. His words bring an immediate smile to my tear-stained face. I've had someone to guide me over the last few months as well. My father, who's been in prison over 30 years for multiple murders, has been very helpful. When Craig realised I was trapped in my marriage to Aaron he offered to sort things out for me through his network of unsavoury contacts. It was tempting but when Jesse offered to step in I decided that was a simpler way to go about things. I believed we'd have less chance of being found out, given neither of us had a criminal record.

As promised, Jesse was true to his word and even though he got caught he didn't reveal the truth about the part I played in events.

So I got away with murder...

The enormity of it all only really began to sink in when I sat down on that narrow plane seat earlier today. I've been so caught up in maintaining my lies that the truth has become a little lost along the way.

But Aaron is dead. And my new life is finally beginning.

Sitting back down on the sofa, I pick up my half-drunk mug of hot chocolate. I thought this would be the perfect place for some respite. There's lots of opportunity for exercise on the slopes but plenty of activities and good food to keep me busy. I also adore the chalet here. It's cosy and just feels more straightforward to be in than the rambling mansion of Burcott House or my equally generously proportioned family home in the adjacent grounds. This ski resort has been my happy place and my escape throughout my marriage to Aaron. I always look forward to being out here and try to get as much time as I can at the resort. Although the opportunities to stay here have lessened in recent years due to the demands of the business and the twins' school, so it's been at least eight months since I was last here. As I entered Snowfall Chalet I felt an instant calm walking through the familiar blue door. What I hadn't reckoned on seeing seconds after I arrived was the family portrait hanging over the fireplace.

I'm staring at it right now. In the photograph, Aaron is smiling widely, his perfectly straight teeth on display, crinkles at the edges of his eyes and his arms thrown around me and Jasper. Our son is also grinning from ear to ear and even Ophelia, who loves to pose, has been caught with genuine laughter on her face. The majority of photographs that I have of the four of us are more formal; so this is unusual because of our casual and carefree demeanours. And it's my own figure that I'm drawn to the most. My head is slightly tilted towards my husband and I'm looking at him, not at the camera. There's an expression of love on my face and it upsets me in a way I couldn't have predicted. I wasn't expecting to shed any tears over him but being here has brought up reminders of how happy we were at the start of our relationship. When did we lose that? Why did our relationship turn sour?

The children must be about five years old in the picture, so it's almost half a decade ago. A lot went on in that time. Aaron changed and I changed. He became more controlling and I became less tolerant of his behaviour. We were both testing boundaries, stretching the limits of our patience with one another. And I snapped first. This is the one thing that helps me justify my actions. Aaron was a ruthless man; I'd seen the way he treated the people he disliked. I knew I had to act before our marriage crumbled completely – because he wouldn't have spared any thought for me if he decided he'd had enough of me.

As it happened, I was just in the nick of time as Aaron had already instigated at least one extramarital affair. I was working against a ticking clock. It was me against him, and I won. I haven't felt truly guilty, until now. Seeing the happy family portrait hanging on the wall of the chalet has stirred up too many memories. Memories of a time when I thought Aaron really loved me and that we'd be together forever.

I look around the room where we spent so much time together. We especially used to love coming to the ski resort when the kids were really small. Juggling twins is a tough gig and, despite Aaron's suggestions, I didn't succumb to employing a round-the-clock nanny. I wanted to do as much as I could myself. But here the resort offers amazing ski lessons for youngsters as soon as they're big enough to walk. Ophelia and Jasper would play for hours out on the snow and then sleep soundly throughout the night because of all the fresh air and exercise they were having. Then the four of us would swim in the plush pool together or take a toboggan ride or go stargazing. Those were the very best times we had together as a family – a far cry from the tense atmosphere at home and the pressure for me and the kids to always be perfect in front of Aaron's friends and family.

I sip my hot chocolate, even though it's cold now, and try to pull my mind away from those thoughts. That way madness lies. I can't look back; I did what I had to and the only way to go is forward.

This is my time now, to create the life that I want to live instead of forever adhering to somebody else's schedule and expectations. I'm going to embrace it and I'm going to squeeze out every moment of happiness that I can. There's just one thing standing between me and my future.

And that's Sasha.

It's her fault that Jesse and I weren't able to become an item. That set off the whole ripple of events that eventually led me to murdering my husband. My sister has made it clear that she still resents me too, even though she doesn't know the full truth. She just believes Jesse has an obsession with me. It's much more than that: we had a full-blown love affair. As an older sister, she's always stood in my way, getting to everything I wanted first, and exactly the same thing happened with Jesse.

She's crossed me one time too many. Jesse doesn't know this – I'm sure he wouldn't approve of my plan to get rid of the mother of his child – but I want Sasha gone too. I want revenge for her stealing the life I should've had with Jesse.

Although Sasha is on the path to self-destruction anyway and, given how much she's drinking, I may not have to do much. So I'm just going to wait and watch, and bide my time...

Chapter Five

Sasha

I wake with a start. The room is in darkness and it must still be the early hours of the morning. A warm little body has slid in beside me and I wrap my arm gratefully around my daughter Freya.

'Mummy, I couldn't sleep,' she says shakily.

'What's the matter sweetheart?' I ask, keeping my voice low as my mum is sound asleep in her bed on the other side of the bedroom. It's a generously proportioned space and my mum's breathing is slow and deep, so our whispered conversation shouldn't cause a disturbance. She's resting so peacefully, despite the chaos of recent events.

Freya doesn't answer me so I say, 'It can be tricky trying to get to sleep in a new place.' I combatted this tonight by sneakily pouring myself another helping of bourbon into my hot chocolate and I also took another straight shot for good measure. This meant I blacked out as soon as my head hit the soft, feather pillow. I feel terrible that my little girl has been lying awake, unable to drift off.

'It's not that,' she explains. Freya pauses for another beat and then says, 'When is Daddy coming home?'

My heart is in my mouth. I've very delicately tried to have this conversation with Freya several times now. She asks when Jesse will be coming home more frequently than I can cope with. The truth is, I don't know. He hasn't had his sentencing yet. The festive period has stalled progress on that front and, even though he's pleading guilty and will therefore get a shorter time period for confessing, he won't be let out of jail until Freya is a grown woman. The thought is depressing. As angry as I am with Jesse, he's a good father. He will be missing Freya like mad and the same goes for her. I just don't know how or why he could entertain risking his daughter's happiness. It just doesn't make sense.

I pull Freya a little closer to me. 'Sweetheart, I'm sorry, we don't know yet. We have to wait to see what's been decided. But... you could send him a letter in the meantime.'

I don't really want to have to have anything to do with Jesse ever again but we're tied to each other through Freya. If she wants to have contact with him, to write to her father, or call him or even go to visit, then I'll support her every step of the way. It'll be hard but there's been enough damage done already and I want Freya to know that Jesse still loves her, even though he's made some very bad mistakes.

I stroke Freya's hair, smoothing it down and singing a little lullaby at the same time. Within minutes, she's snuggled asleep in my arms. I smile to myself; she may be growing up but she'll always be my baby. I'm glad she's here with me, because I can't get used to being in bed alone. That's one of the reasons for my late-night drinking. Somehow going to bed without Jesse's solid form being there next to me is the worst part of the day. I feel lonely and confused. Questions keep circling my mind, the main one being: why is this happening to our family?

I don't know how we can ever get back to normal life. I'm not sure I can return to my job as an assistant headteacher or face my friends or my neighbours ever again. Jesse has obliterated any confidence I had and he's blown up every aspect of our lives. Parents from Freya's school initially sent messages to say they were sorry to hear about what I was going through but I've heard nothing from anyone since that first flurry. And when I contacted the mother of Freya's best friend to arrange a playdate before our holiday, to give my daughter some normalcy, the mother's response was she couldn't allow her child to be friends with Freya anymore, not after what Jesse did. And that wasn't all, an egg was thrown at our front window, my postman refuses to say hello now and even my closest friend is freezing me out and not taking my calls. What Jesse did will impact me and Freya for the rest of our lives.

I try to push these thoughts out of my mind, but it's no good; once I've started on this train of thinking I can't stop. So I carefully untangle myself from Freya's arms and then hurry into the kitchen and grab the vodka from the drinks cupboard. I down a shot, and then another and another. Making myself place the bottle back where it came from, I stagger along the hallway and roll back under the covers. My mind is relaxed again now and sleep claims me once more.

***

'Mummy, Mummy, it's time to wake up!' Freya is shaking me urgently but, despite her insistence, I'm finding it difficult to move. My limbs feel heavy and my mouth tastes like cardboard.

'Urgh, I heard you,' I respond groggily. 'Give Mummy a minute.'

I roll over and pull the covers up round my ears, but Freya persists.

'Come on now, breakfast is ready,' Freya bosses. 'You're going to miss it.'

Eating is the last thing I want to do right now, but I know it's important to try to keep my body in some sort of routine so, with much effort, I heave myself out of bed and allow my daughter to propel me into the communal room.

'Good morning, love,' my mum says in a cheerful voice. 'Would you like bacon?'

My stomach churns in response. 'No!' My voice is snappier than I intended. 'No thanks, just a coffee for me.'

'You can't just have coffee for breakfast,' my mum chides. 'At least have some dry toast for starters.'

I'm almost forty years old and yet my mum still fusses around me like I'm five. I nod in response and allow her to furnish me with a cup of black coffee and a plain, unbuttered piece of toast.

I take in the rest of the breakfast bar: my mum has gone to town this morning with scrambled eggs, hash browns, mushrooms, fried tomatoes and baked beans to go with the toast and bacon. She's cooked up a full English, despite the fact everyone has been eating more food than usual over Christmas. Personally, I've gone right off food and the thought of consuming such a vast amount makes me recoil back a few steps. I take a seat on one of the low, leather armchairs in the lounge area of the open-plan room instead of positioning myself at the breakfast bar.

'We're all going to need our energy today,' Nadia says pointedly, looking at me. 'Skiing is excellent exercise but it burns a lot of calories, so we need to set ourselves up properly.'

I groan internally at this remark. Erin has booked us all onto ski lessons today which is the last thing I want to do. I'm out of sorts after the journey here and I could do with a day to recharge before the physical exertion. The three children are booked onto a children's club for the whole day while Leah, Mum and I have a five-hour intensive 'introduction to the slopes' lesson. Leah has zero experience of the sport while me and mum are confident skiing on artificial snow but have never skied on a mountain before. Erin gave us lots of options for the various sessions we could do and we could've all split up and done courses tailored to our specific abilities, but mum decided she wanted the three of us to stick together so this lesson was broad enough to work for us all. Erin has been skiing at this resort for years so she's not in need of any training at all. She'll be hitting the slopes on her own today.

'Can I have some more bacon?' Jasper pipes up.

'Of course you can,' my mum beams, pleased that someone is making the most of her cooking.

Erin has finished her breakfast, Leah already has a full face of make-up, and even the children are already dressed and raring to go.

I take a small bite out of the toast and chew slowly.

'We've only got half an hour until we leave,' Erin announces. 'We need some time to get between here and the meeting point for the ski lessons, so chop chop, everyone!'

Erin can plainly see I'm nowhere near ready and the idea of rushing around to get out of the door makes me want to weep. But then I look at Freya's excited face and it's the motivation I need to sort myself out. I gulp down the coffee and leave the remains of the toast discarded on the plate on the wooden coffee table before hurrying to my bedroom to throw on some clothes and comb my unruly hair. Perhaps the exercise today will be good for me. And I must admit the idea of skiing on real snow interests me more than anything else has in the last month. I don't feel physically prepared for today but the thought of being out on the mountainside is the closest I've come to being excited, or curious, or optimistic since Jesse's arrest. My emotions have felt dulled like I'm now living life in greyscale instead of full colour.

As I pull my skiwear from my suitcase, images of Jesse and I at the snow centre near to where we live flood my mind. Jesse and I used to go quite a bit on a Friday evening for a date night or at the weekend when Freya was over at her friend's house. There's a dry ski slope section as well as some slopes with artificial snow on. I enjoyed learning to ski on but we never had the money for a skiing holiday. So it's a little bit ironic that we're here now as Jesse would've been in his element. I shake the thoughts of him away and hop into the shower for a quick wash.

By the time I'm sorted, everyone else is waiting expectantly by the front door. Erin's eyebrows are raised in annoyance. My pulse rate speeds up: I hate the feeling of being late. I want to retaliate but I don't, I just say, 'Sorry, all good to go,' with as much enthusiasm as I can muster.

Freya's little hand slips into mine. 'We're going to have a brilliant day!' She smiles at me.

'Yes, we are,' I agree and squeeze her fingers between mine. I've got to keep going for her, just placing one foot in front of the other until things start to feel a little easier. I've got to try to put Jesse and Aaron and everything that happened at that Christmas party behind me, for my daughter's sake.

I just hope I can do it.

Chapter Six

Leah

'You won't get much better snow than here,' Erin says proudly, as though she was somehow involved in creating the quality of it. I have no idea what 'good' snow is because I'm not an experienced skier. However, I could easily get used to this lifestyle. I'm soaking up the atmosphere, which is charged with energy and laughter, and plenty of conversations swirl around us as we enter the ski village. This is the meeting point for our initial ski lessons and I can't wait to put my own skis on.

Despite never having skied before, I'm kitted out like a pro. That's because I got in touch with a ski wear brand and told them about my trip. They responded by sending out a whole wardrobe of designer ski wear for me to try out while I'm here. In return, I have to post regular social media content showing pictures and videos of me wearing their clothing range. I was very happy with the arrangement as it saved me the job of having to shop for appropriate outfits. Remembering this, I whip out my phone and grab a quick selfie of me entering the ski village, my brightly coloured jacket and the ski goggles atop my head visible in the image.

Erin gives us a tour of the shopping centre, the restaurants, and the bars. I can't believe how much there is here. I've been told this is one of the largest ski resorts, but I didn't realise how much could be on offer on this type of getaway. At least it means there's plenty for me to do if I don't get on with the actual skiing itself.

'Time for your lessons,' Erin announces to the three children and guides them to the place where their instructor and a number of others their age are gathering.

Jasper bounds ahead. He's not usually super confident but he loves sports so it's nice to see him so eager. Ophelia struts into the cluster of children and waves at another girl, perhaps someone she already knows. Freya, who's usually an extrovert, hangs back and clings to Sasha's side. It's not like her to behave like this but it's a completely new environment for her. She's skied on dry slopes with her parents but not on a mountain so she must be feeling overwhelmed. Jasper and Ophelia have been skiing since they were tiny tots so I hope they'll help Freya while she's learning.

Sasha bends down and whispers a few things in Freya's ear. In response, Freya gives Sasha a big hug before joining the other two. They're all so alike and close in age that Freya could easily be mistaken for a third sibling or even a triplet next to her two cousins. It's interesting watching the trio interact – they're already so familiar with each other. It's as though they've known each other their whole lives, which isn't the case. Freya was only introduced to the twins at the Christmas party last month. It feels like such a long time ago now, and we've all spent so much time with each other since, so it's no wonder Freya has already formed a bond with Jasper and Ophelia. Sometimes extreme circumstances can bring people closer together, so I hope the friendship of a new generation of Baileys will be something positive to come out of the last few weeks.

'Let's go and get a drink in the observatory café,' Erin suggests. 'We can watch them for half an hour before your own session begins.'

I'm all for this but I can tell Sasha is feeling nervous about leaving Freya.

'Come on,' I encourage. 'You'll have a better view from up high by the sounds of it.'

Sasha nods and allows me to loop an arm through hers. We find some seats and settle down to watch Jasper, Ophelia and Freya as they get to grips with their skis. Jasper is off the minute the instructor finishes his briefing, pushing himself easily forward. It's nice to catch sight of his wide smile as he goes. Ophelia follows him, a look of determination on her face. It's easy to see she wants to overtake her brother at the first opportunity and I'm glued to the pair of them battling it out. Ophelia does get ahead of Jasper after a couple of minutes – she's so like her mother Erin.

Freya is wobbling on her own skis. This makes me apprehensive for when it's my turn. Maybe I should just stick to observing rather than participating. I'm loving the vibe in the café. The scent of cinnamon and coffee drift in the air around me and the large suede armchair wraps around me like a warm hug. I lean back against the soft material of the head rest just as I witness Freya topple over. Her face crumples as she goes down and I jerk forward again to see if she's okay.

'Oh!' Sasha exclaims beside me.

'She'll get there,' Mom, sitting on the other side of Sasha, says reassuringly.

I'm about to settle back into the chair when I hear someone call my name. Twisting round, I see a tall figure advancing towards me. They're kitted out head to toe in ski wear with their visor still down.

I have absolutely no idea who this person is and why they're coming towards me. My heart thumps faster. Is this the anonymous messenger? Or the obsessive stalker who just won't leave me alone? Maybe my past has finally caught up with me...

I leap up, wanting to put as much space as possible between me and whoever this is.

'Leah, it's me.'

The visor comes down to reveal sandy-coloured hair, a dimpled chin and sea-blue eyes.

I laugh.

The tension in my body immediately releases. For a few brief seconds I thought I might be in danger. Instead, a very handsome man is standing before me. Xavier Knight has materialised just as I hoped he would. When we met at Erin's Christmas party over a month ago, I was keen for us to see each other again. With everything that went on in the aftermath of Aaron's death – the police questioning, the late nights and emotions running high between the Bailey women – there hasn't been much opportunity to ignite things. I saw Xavier only briefly at the sombre, tense funeral that we had for Aaron last week. Mom and Sasha decided it was best to stay away out of respect or Aaron's family. After all, Sasha is Jesse's wife and they may have been upset by her presence. But Erin asked me to go along for moral support. I was worried someone might object to me being there as well, tarnished by my association with Sasha and Jesse, but thankfully no one said a word and I left the wake early with Erin as she wasn't up to staying for long. I spoke to Xavier for a fleeting half an hour but my head wasn't really in our conversation.

Erin has told me previously that the Knight family go way back with Aaron's family – the Scott's – and traditionally have coordinated their skiing trips so I'm glad that things have synced up for this trip. According to Erin, Aaron's father has decided not to come out so soon after his son's death. But Xavier's mother and sister are flying here to join him next week as usual. From what I've heard, Xavier genuinely sounds like an all-round good guy and, judging by the way he's looking at me, I think he's just as interested in me as I am in him.

'You are rocking that outfit, Leah!' He winks at me. I'm secretly pleased that I selected the best of my ski wear ensembles to wear today – a lavender all-in-one suit that nips in neatly at the waist.

'Likewise,' I shoot back at him. He's wearing a matching dark black ski jacket and trousers, with slashes of bright orange colour that contrasts in an eye-catching way.

'Erin, how are you?' Xavier swivels his attention to my sister, who has just moved to stand next to me.

'It's early days,' Erin says demurely and casts her eyes downwards.

'I'm pleased to see you've come out for the snow, I'm sure it'll do you good.'

'I hope so... It'll be good for the children after being cooped up for the past few weeks,' Erin responds.

Xavier leans in and gives her a hug. It's bad enough when you lose a loved one, especially a spouse, but to lose them in such an untimely and distressing way is unimaginable. There have been so many awkward exchanges for Erin as people really don't know what to say to her at the moment. But Xavier has handled the conversation as smoothly as possible.

'What are your plans?' Xavier asks us.

Erin is looking down again, twisting her wedding ring on her finger so I reply instead. 'I'm going to be taking some lessons.'

Xavier is about to say something when another skier comes to a halt next to him.

'Ah, there you are.' Xavier pats the man on the back. 'This is Fernando, he's a university friend who's come out for the week.'

'Hi.' Fernando raises his hand in greeting. He smiles at me but his eyes don't reach mine. They're riveted somewhere below my chin. I shudder and immediately label him as a sleazeball.

'Actually, we're thinking of going for a drink tonight,' Xavier says. 'Would you like to join us?'

Erin immediately declines but encourages me to go.

'I'd love to,' I accept.

'Great, meet you at The Ice Bar at eight p.m.?'

'Perfect, see you there.'

Xavier and Fernando nod their goodbyes and leave. A little frisson of excitement sizzles through me. Is this a date? Is this the start of something with Xavier? I'm immediately mentally running through my wardrobe options for the evening and selecting a casual yet figure-hugging outfit for the occasion. For the first time in ages, I'm into a guy who seems decent.

A part of me had been dreading this winter getaway. But now there's something to look forward to.

Perhaps this trip isn't going to be so bad after all...

Chapter Seven

Nadia

I watch the broad-shouldered, attractive young male walk away and a tremor runs down my spine. I've got a bad feeling about Xavier Knight's interest in Leah. Perhaps it's just paranoia, as a result of Sasha and Erin's romantic choices, or maybe it's a mother's instinct, but I don't trust him. Not one little bit.

He's extremely polished and utterly charming, I'll give him that. However, that's potentially where my concerns begin as well. He reminds me too much of Erin's deceased husband. Like Aaron, Xavier is born of privileged stock. He's from an exceptionally wealthy family and used to getting exactly what he wants. And the thing he wants at the moment is my youngest daughter.

I blow out a breath. I used to think that once my daughters hit eighteen that would be it. End of all parental worries. But the exact opposite has occurred. I worry about them more as adults than I ever did as children. When they were younger they were either with me or at school for the most part. I knew exactly what they were doing, who they were with, and that their environments were safe. Now, any one of them can be anywhere in the world doing all manner of things that set my nerves jangling. Leah, with her bungee jumps and deep-sea diving, has given me more cause for anxiety than I ever imagined. I was on tenterhooks the whole time Sasha was pregnant with Freya. And I endured ten long years of estrangement with Erin, worrying and wondering what was going on with her. It turns out, on paper, she had the perfect life: an enviable home and business, two cute kids and a wealthy husband. Except I've gleaned from things she's said that she didn't have the easiest marriage. Aaron liked to be in control, which must have been difficult for Erin as she's always been so independent.

As Erin directs us towards our own skiing lessons, my brain is whirring. The last thing this family needs is another good-looking male disrupting the balance and distracting from this holiday, which is meant to be a time for us all to refresh and relax. I look at Leah, walking beside me with a bounce in her step, and decide that I need to intervene and stop her going out to see Xavier tonight. I know she's not a teenager anymore and she can make her own mind up about who she dates but Xavier just feels all wrong. He was a friend of Aaron's and a connection to Erin's husband that we could do without.

'Are you OK, Mom?' Leah asks me quizzically.

'Yes...' I begin, before changing my mind. 'Actually no, I'm feeling quite tired. I was hoping we could all curl up in front of a movie after dinner, with some popcorn. Like we used to do in the old days.'

Leah smiles. 'That would be great.'

I exhale. It's possible Leah isn't as interested in Xavier as I'd thought and is going to be easily dissuaded from meeting up with him.

'There should be time to watch something before I go out this evening.'

My stomach drops. So she is keen to see Xavier then. I'm going to have to think of something more convincing to keep her in tonight.

'Here we are,' Erin announces as we pitch up for our lesson.

'Which slope are you going to hit first?' I ask my middle daughter.

'Oh, the hardest one – of course!' She gives me a smile, her perfect white teeth on display.

To the outside world anyone would believe me to be a proud mother, and I am in many ways. Erin has always been ambitious and she's managed to break into a completely different world of high-value houses, winter holidays and an endless supply of money. But I know what she's capable of and I've witnessed first-hand how devious she can be. A mother's love is infinite and, even though I'm fully aware of the flaws she masks and the lies she hides with her fancy clothes and sweet-smelling perfume, I still hold onto the idea that I can help Erin to change the path she's on. The mistakes she's made are irreversible but I've vowed to stick by her side, to steer her into becoming a better person and to make sure she doesn't repeat her past behaviours.

But there's something about the hurried way in which Erin checks her watch and the impatient flick of her gaze in the direction that we've just come from that has me questioning whether she's going to ski today or if my middle daughter has other plans entirely.

As Erin leaves, I tell myself to remove all thoughts of Leah's potential date this evening, Freya's struggles to adapt to life without her father, Sasha's drinking problem and Erin's scheming out of my head as I try to lose myself in the thrill of skiing once again. The excitement of being on real snow, and the exhilaration that follows as I carve my path down my first descent, temporarily wipes away my worries and briefly sets my soul alight.

I came to skiing late – I could never have afforded such an affluent hobby in my younger days. But Sasha and Jesse got me a voucher for an experience day at our local ski centre for my sixtieth and I was surprised to find I loved it. I kept going with the lessons, as a retirement hobby, and joined a group for people of a similar age who meet once a fortnight for regular skiing sessions. It's been a dream of mine to ski on proper snow. I was hoping to book a trip with my friends Gilly and Helga but we've never quite got round to arranging it.

Sasha comes down the slope behind me and I observe that she's not got her usual control over her skis. It then takes her several attempts to mount the ski lift. I tighten my grip on my ski poles; Sasha's uncharacteristically erratic behaviour is a major cause of angst for me and I'm planning to have a heart-to-heart with her to discuss how she's coping – or rather not coping. The awful end to her marriage with Jesse has rocked Sasha's world, that's for sure. It's not been easy on any of us.

As I swoop down the slope for a second time, I'm reminded that Jesse always encouraged me to better myself where health and fitness were concerned. There were a lot of perks to having a son-in-law who essentially acted as my own personal trainer, and I've got him to thank for my toned physique. I know I'm much stronger and fitter because of his guidance. It's just one of the many ways that Jesse shaped our lives and my heart twinges with sadness when I think about the summer afternoon rounders games we had as a family, the walks we used to go on in all weathers and the evenings Jesse, Sasha and I spent together working out in the make-shift gym Jesse set up in the garage of his marital home. Jesse wasn't perfect and I always had a close eye on him because I knew about the first time he and Erin had an affair. But, over time, we grew to have a generally positive relationship. In the early years, I was wary that he'd stray again but he stuck by Sasha and doted on little Freya. I'd been concerned that he and Sasha were going through a rough patch recently, but I never thought he would cheat again after all this time. But it's true what they say — a leopard never really changes its spots. I simultaneously miss him as a member of my brood whilst also wanting to scream at him for ripping my family apart.

The glacial air and incredible mountain backdrop are wonderfully atmospheric – and a much-needed distraction. For a second time I instruct myself to stop worrying and just concentrate on the movement of my body. As I glide through the snow, my muscles get into a rhythm and I don't even have to think about what I'm doing. I'm already raring to go and the instructor praises me on my technique. I know I'll need to work my way up to it but I'm already daydreaming about the more challenging slopes to come.

A number of hours fly by and the time I'm spending out in the open gives me a renewed sense of hope and purpose. Sometimes being outside is just what we need to take ourselves out of our trials and tribulations.

Suddenly Sasha shoots past me, going far too fast.

'Sasha, careful!' I yell just before she crashes into another skier and lands in a tangle on the snow.

I speed towards her and arrive at her side just as the instructor reaches the two felled people.

'All fine,' Sasha tells me immediately. Her cheeks are flushed with embarrassment. 'I'm so sorry,' she garbles to the other skier.

'No harm done,' the other woman says primly, before skiing off in a different direction.

The ski instructor heaves Sasha to her feet.

'Perhaps you could do with a break?' I suggest.

'It's time to finish up now anyway,' the instructor says to us before heading off to round up everyone else in the group..

Thankfully, we were already near the starting point of the slope and the ski village isn't too far for Sasha to hobble to. I help Sasha out of her skis and then loop my arm around her waist. Then we slowly make our way to the warmth of the ski centre.

'Does anything hurt?'

Sasha shakes her head and wriggles out of my arms.

'I know it didn't end so well, but did you manage to have a good time? I thought that was fun,' I say as brightly as I can as I climb out of my own skis.

Sasha shrugs her shoulders nonchalantly just as Leah catches up with us. She had stuck to the smallest slopes during the session where another instructor was guiding complete beginners.

'That was brilliant!' she enthuses. 'I can't wait to get back out here tomorrow.'

I agree with Leah and we chatter animatedly as we make our way to the collection point for the children. Erin is waiting there already and it strikes me that she doesn't look flushed or ruffled like the rest of us. Her outfit is still pristine and her shining copper locks are immaculate. The hairs on the back of my neck prickle with suspicion but I let it go and make a mental note to find out how Erin has really spent her time today.

Jasper comes bounding back to us and the little boy is all smiles. But the same can't be said for Ophelia and Freya.

Freya rushes towards us, tears streaming down her face, and dives straight into a surprised Sasha's arms. Ophelia is hot on her heels, her cheeks are also streaked with tears, but she's boiling hot with anger as well.

'Whatever's the matter?' I ask.

'Your daddy killed my daddy!' Ophelia shouts, pointing her finger at Freya.

A few people standing nearby turn to look at us curiously, to see if there's any truth in the words of the red-haired girl. I scowl at them, making it clear their interest is not wanted.

Sasha is trembling and Leah is standing agape. Even Erin, who is usually cool and collected, has gone white with astonishment.

'Now, now,' I say, taking charge of the situation. 'Lower your voice Ophelia, this is not something to be discussed in public. Let's get back to the chalet.'

'Actually, I'm going to take Ophelia with me for a bit,' Erin responds firmly. 'I think it's best if I talk with her separately first. Jasper, do you want to come with us?'

Jasper takes one look at his emotional sister and shakes his head. 'I'll go with Grandmother.'

I really wish the twins wouldn't refer to me so formally but I'm pleased they're both becoming more comfortable around me — and that Jasper is happy to come with me now.

'It's OK, he can walk back with me. You take as long as you need.'

Erin quickly ushers Ophelia away, the youngster's eyes still glittering with fury.

Freya continues to cry uncontrollably in Sasha's arms but, slowly, we make our way back to the chalet. Once we're there, emotions calm down and I rustle up some omelettes and chips for everyone. Jasper is hungry after this morning's excursions and he's first to the table, shovelling chips into his mouth like only a nine-year-old can.

'Dinner!' I call. Leah drifts to join us and half-heartedly stabs away at the food on her plate. But Sasha and Freya are in one of the bedrooms and, as the minutes tick by, there's no sign of them joining us.

I push my own food around my plate, my fears for my family increasing ten-fold. I can't shake Ophelia's words from my head and the way she looked as she exploded earlier on.

Your daddy killed my daddy!

With Jesse's trial coming up, I worry that it will be impossible to keep the events leading up to Aaron's murder a secret. And, for the first time, I wonder if I will be able to keep the terrible truth about his death buried...

Because I know the part Erin played in her husband's death. I saw it happen.

Will we ever put this nightmare behind us?

Chapter Eight

Erin

'Mummy, it's true! Freya's daddy *did* kill my daddy!'

Ophelia's voice is high-pitched and her whole body is trembling. I'm stunned by her words, mostly because they're true. I reach out for her and we walk hand in hand, away from the rest of our family. Ophelia falls silent and I'm temporarily lost in my thoughts.

One thing I hadn't fully thought about when Jesse and I were set on our path to get rid of Aaron was the impact on my children. I admit this was partly for selfish reasons and my need to escape my claustrophobic marriage. But it was also because Aaron was forever away at business conferences or stuck in the office until late at night. And, as I discovered recently, he was busy conducting an affair with a member of our staff at the hotel – raven-haired waitress Nia. So Ophelia and Jasper barely saw him during the school week. He did make the effort to spend a bit more time with them at weekends, but only if it didn't interfere with his golf tournaments. I guess, because Aaron was such a fleeting presence in our lives, I hadn't appreciated the depth of my children's feelings for him or how the nature of his passing would affect them.

Alongside that, the man I thought was my biological father died when I was eight. Yes, it was tough but my mother was always the constant in my life and I've always been independent. I guess the premature death of the man I called Daddy taught me early on that you can only rely on yourself - and that life is very uncertain. It's a lesson my children are starting to learn too.

Ophelia tugs on my arm and brings me back to the present.

'Ophelia, I know it's hard to understand but you really can't go around shouting those kinds of things in public. And it wasn't right for Freya to find out like that.'

Ophelia pouts. 'But it was OK for me to hear Leah and Sasha talking about it at Christmastime?'

'No, that wasn't OK either.'

A flash of annoyance bubbles inside me. Ophelia overheard my two sisters discussing her father's death and she's right, that was no way for her to discover that Jesse pushed Aaron to his death. I'd wanted to whisk her straight off for counselling but my mother insisted we deal with things as a family. That was several weeks ago though and it's been a long time for Ophelia to keep things to herself. We were planning to sit down with the children and explain things gently to them on this trip. But Ophelia has had her feelings bottled up for too long and it's apparent now that she was going to burst at some point. In hindsight, I'm just surprised it hasn't happened before now. I've been so preoccupied with Aaron's funeral and sorting out all the paperwork that goes with making someone's exit from this world official that time has slipped by too fast. I should've dealt with my children's emotions as my first priority.

I give Ophelia a squeeze. 'Look, we're going to get you some proper help to cope with everything,' I promise. 'But you can't blame Freya for what happened. She has nothing to do with it and she wants to be your friend.'

Ophelia huffs at me. I crouch down and look into her green eyes. 'Sweetie, trust me, things will get better. We can talk more about this together as well. Just, please, don't be mad at Freya.'

Ophelia still doesn't look as though she's convinced.

'Would you want Freya to be mad at you for something I'd done?' I ask.

I realise as I'm saying this that if the truth came out, then Ophelia could very well be in this position.

She shakes her head.

'Exactly. Let Freya be your friend, she's a good girl and it's important you two stick together.' I kiss her on the cheek and straighten up. I've grown to like Freya over the past few weeks, she's smart and full of energy. In many ways she reminds me of myself as a child.

'Oh, look! Over there!' The dark cloud has quickly passed from Ophelia's face and she's now standing eagerly on her tiptoes.

'An ice rink!' we both echo in unison.

'Go on then.' I smile at her. 'We can have a quick skate around the rink.'

I may be hard-hearted when it comes to most people but my kids aren't included in that. They really are the two human beings I love most on this earth. Ever since they were growing in my stomach, my drive has been to create a perfect life for them. To give them everything I didn't have in my own childhood and set them on a path for the future that's beyond my wildest dreams. So when they ask me for something that I know will make them happy, I find it difficult to resist.

We make our way towards the brightly lit ice rink. It's not too busy with just a smattering of people weaving around the edges. We get our ice-skates on speedily; I'm just as impatient to get on the rink as my daughter is.

The blades on the bottom of my boot connect with the smooth ice and I skim the hard surface. Ophelia has donned her warm gloves and her woolly hand grasps mine. One foot in front of the other, we move in tandem, easily picking up a rhythm.

'I love being on the ice, Mummy,' Ophelia says next to me, sounding a million times happier than she was half an hour ago.

I know what I'm doing is a distraction technique and I'm going to have to have a proper conversation with Ophelia about her father's murder and Jesse's upcoming trial. But, right now, I just want to treasure this snapshot in time with my little girl. For me, this holiday is an escape from everything that's happened and I'm going to embrace it while we're here.

Ophelia lets go of me just as the music system switches on. An upbeat pop song blares out of the speakers and my daughter soars across the ice rink, twirling in the middle before racing back to me. She's always been obsessed with winter sports. Out here she thrives when she's on the snow but she loves the ice just as much. And she's getting really good, her balance is near-perfect and she has no fear. She trusts her body and its ability to move in the way she directs it to. I hope she never loses that confidence.

I clap. 'Bravo! That was excellent!'

Ophelia urges me to copy her and I don't take much persuading. Being in the midst of the majestic French Alps and able to take advantage of all that's on offer at this incredible ski resort is not something

I take for granted. This is everything I've worked for and I appreciate it all. Because I know just how fast it could all be taken away from me. It happened to my husband, and I'm under no illusion that my world could come crashing down at any moment. They say money can buy you anything you want but what a lot of wealth won't do is buy you piece of mind. Because the more you have, the more you stand to lose.

After another twenty minutes we're both breathless so I call time and we head back to our chalet. Ophelia appears calmer and she's agreed to not say anything more about it to Freya. We've scheduled an evening later in the week to have dinner together, just the two of us. And that's when I'll talk things through with my daughter.

I take in her flowing red hair and cute button nose; she's almost ten now and I know both of my children are going to do a lot of growing up in this next year. Even more so as we adjust to being a family of three. Ophelia entwines her gloved fingers with my own and we walk in a companionable silence.

As we near the chalet, darkness has fallen and my shoulders feel heavy with the burden of all this pretence. My mind is in conflict. On the one hand, I want to have the perfect family trip but the reality of that means spending a lot of time with my mother, Sasha and Leah. Of the three of them, Leah is the only person I trust. She's the most open and honest one of all the Bailey women. My mother is all kinds of complicated and she's also very clever. And Sasha is a problem I'm planning to deal with. But, as the saying goes, you keep your friends close and your enemies closer. I need all three of them where I can keep an eye on them.

Because my mother knows the truth about my part in Aaron's death. I can't risk her going rogue and ruining everything. My bet is she wouldn't do that to me. We spent ten years apart and I don't think she wants that to happen again. I can't be sure though – she turned on me once and she may do it again. So I've got to keep my guard up and ensure she has no reason to betray me and every reason to do what I want. It helps that I've now got a huge amount of wealth at my disposal. I know this trip means a lot to her, not just because it's family time together but because it's been her dream to come on a skiing trip. I'm guessing this is going to go a long way to keeping her sweet.

Outside the chalet, I almost jump out of my skin. There's a face staring out of the window, blank and devoid of emotion. It takes me a split second to realise it's Sasha. She looks so drawn and so unlike herself. She's barely eaten in the past few weeks and it's starting to show. Instead, she's been drinking plenty, drowning her sorrows, and the effects of that are becoming apparent.

My hatred for Sasha still burns hot after all these years. We've always disliked each other, even as children. We're so close in age that we were constantly squabbling and arguing. That pattern continued into our teenage years and then into our early adulthood as well. Our mother always used to say the reason we clashed was because we're so alike, but I don't think that's the case.

For me, I always felt like Sasha was elbowing me out the way to get what she wanted. She got to keep Jesse, he stayed with her and didn't confess to his love affair with me the first time round because Sasha was pregnant with Freya. Sasha still doesn't know the truth. Our mother found out and made Jesse and I swear we'd never tell Sasha that we had feelings for each other. After Jesse's arrest at the party, Sasha was led to believe he was infatuated with me. I'm going to relish the day when I finally reveal to her that her whole married life was a lie. I'm not even going to feel a little bit guilty.

After all, Sasha also made our entire family turn against me in the aftermath of Leah's accident ten years ago. I allowed my emotions about Jesse to get the better of me and that's ultimately the reason why I was upset when I was behind the wheel of the car that crashed into my little sister. When Leah was in hospital, Sasha was unrelenting in the way she blamed me for that accident and just kept sticking the knife in. And twisting it again and again. It was her behaviour and the weight of keeping my feelings for Jesse secret that made me leave and I will never forgive her for that.

'In you go,' I say to Ophelia, propelling her through the front door. 'I won't be a minute.'

Ophelia slips into the warmth and I close the blue door shut. I just need a breather before I have to put another performance on. I'm finding it harder to keep all the plates spinning than I thought. Keeping a secret as big as being involved in a murder plot is also difficult to live out day by day. And I'm feeling more and more guilt, as well as more regret over what happened to Aaron. I think it's being here, seeing his portrait and reliving the memories of this place. I'm going to have to take the canvas down because I can't keep looking at his face every time I'm in the chalet.

I give myself a pep talk and then roll my shoulders, in an attempt to loosen my tight muscles. As I do, the porch light flickers on, casting a glow around the front of the building. I'm about to put my key back in the lock when something catches my eye.

I half-turn and then blink in disbelief. I can't believe what I'm seeing. Is this message meant for me? Or was this intended for someone else?

Just mere metres from me are five words scrawled out in the snow. I swallow hard as I read them again, but the bile still rises up in my throat.

I KNOW IT WAS YOU.

Chapter Nine

Sasha

Staring out of the window, my mind and body feel numb. The alcohol is helping with this but, truthfully, I have no idea what I should be thinking or feeling right now. It's like my ability to tap into my emotions has been removed. I can't tell sadness from anger or grief. Everything is just bubbling below the murky surface, all blending into one. I wonder if I will ever feel normal again.

It occurs to me that I could've gone to the doctor to get some medical help. But where would I start in explaining this? And could I face the slight recoil or the expression of pity that came my way when I told the person sitting across the stark, clinical table that my husband is a murderer?

No, I couldn't.

I already had a stash of sleeping pills prescribed. I was suffering with anxiety because of my high-stress and high-demand role as an assistant headteacher. That was nowhere near as stressful as the situation I now find myself in. It's all relative though. At least I was really feeling something then, even if it was often panic and overwhelm. It says something that I'd go back in time to experience those emotions again. Over the last few days my energy levels have dropped dramatically. I guess it could just be my brain's way of trying to give me a rest.

There's a hive of activity behind me. A movie night is being set up and it's perked Freya up enormously. She and I had a cuddle when we first returned to the chalet but the traces of her sadness are gone now. The tear stains on her cheeks are the only sign she was upset. I shift my position at the window and watch her snuggle down underneath a cosy throw, curling her body into Leah's as the TV is switched on.

I force myself to go and join them. Jasper gets to the sofa before me and climbs into the spot immediately next to Freya, dunking his hand into the popcorn pot. Ophelia has already gone to her room and Erin has retired for an early night as well. Ophelia was calmer when she entered the chalet and I wondered what Erin said to dampen the flames of her anger. I'm relieved that she's away from Freya for a bit because I don't want the two of them falling out again this evening.

I perch on the end of the squishy sofa, feeling removed from the conversation about movie choices. My mind remains weirdly blank and I take another sip from my reusable water bottle, which is filled with vodka and orange juice.

Freya and Jasper debate the genre of film for a full ten minutes before finally settling on a compromise.

'I'm glad you got there guys, because I'm going out again in two hours!' Leah jokes with them.

'We didn't take that long, Auntie Leah,' Freya responds.

'Yes you did, I thought you were going to turn ten before you decided!'

I flick my eyes across to my daughter as she giggles at Leah's teasing. I can't believe my baby is turning ten tomorrow. She's going into double digits – how did that happen? It feels like only yesterday that I was rocking her in the crook of my arm, singing lullabies to try and get her to sleep. The last few years have flown by in a haze of juggling work and life, with Freya increasingly out at a friend's house, school discos or one of her many after-school clubs.

'It's cold out there,' my mum is saying to Leah. 'Why don't you stay in with us instead of going back out again?'

Leah gives a giggly response, it's plain to see she's about to get swept up into a romance with Xavier. I tune out the rest of the conversation, not wanting to listen to the hope and giddiness in Leah's voice. It feels like a very long time ago since I was dating Jesse and it hurts too much to cast my mind back to that time, when I was full of optimism and fizzing feelings for the man I fell in love with.

Leah turns down the overhead light and I allow myself to sink into the sofa a little more. I'm trying to stay in the present rather than dwelling too much on the past, but it's easier said than done. I concentrate on the thought that I need to make Freya's birthday tomorrow special. She deserves to have a happy tenth birthday. I think about all the things I want to do with her – opening presents, snuggles by the fire and singing happy birthday. But my mind wanders to the realisation that I'm also going to need to keep her distracted from the reality that Jesse isn't around to celebrate with her.

I picture him cooped up in a small prison cell. He's always been so full of life; I can't imagine how he is coping being in such constrained conditions. Jesse loved being outdoors – cycling, paddleboarding, climbing mountains – and if he wasn't at the gym, he was in a forest somewhere or swimming in the sea. He'll be absolutely gutted not to be celebrating this milestone with his little girl. And there will be many more events throughout our daughter's childhood that he will miss from this point on. I feel a pang of sadness for the family we once were and for the husband I have lost. But I can't wallow in pity for him, not after what he did. Jesse should've thought about the consequences.

As I stare blankly at the TV screen, I still can't quite comprehend that Jesse – my partner of over ten years – is a killer. He's never even got into a fight in the whole time we've been together. He may be muscly after all the hours he's put in at the gym, but he's not the aggressive type. I try to tune into the movie, to direct my thoughts away from the mess my life is in.

My concentration is shot to pieces though, so, instead, I let my gaze fall on Freya. She's laughing at all the appropriate points in the film and looks untroubled. I'm hoping the argument between her and Ophelia was a brief clash rather than the start of difficulties between the two of them. Freya is an only child, so I feel it's important for her to have a positive relationship with her new-found cousins and I'm determined Jesse's actions won't ruin that as well.

The film goes by in a blur and as the credits roll down the screen, mum starts pestering Leah not to go out again. She's reminding her that it's Freya's birthday tomorrow but Leah is digging her heels in and determined to meet Xavier. My mum's insistence is odd and I wonder why she's nagging Leah like she's a teenager. Old habits are hard to shake I guess. They have a bit of back and forth about it but in the end my mum relents and takes Freya off to bed.

'Goodnight my nine-year-old!' I call after her. 'It's going to be a big day tomorrow!' But the door clicks shut and I'm not sure if my daughter heard me or not.

Once my mum is out of the room, Leah slips out the chalet door for her date with Xavier. I'm left alone and so I decide to get started on making some muffins for Freya. I know Mum has already made a pretty pink birthday cake; she's an amazing baker so nothing I do is going to taste quite so delicious. I want to make something as well though so I wash my hands in the butler sink and roll up the sleeves of my checked flannel shirt. I begin by lining up the ingredients in a neat row on the sideboard and then set to work pouring each of them into the bowl. It won't take me long as I've made Freya's favourite chocolate muffin recipe a million times.

Whisking the mixture and then doling out even amounts into the little muffin cases I've placed onto the baking tray feels somehow soothing. I lose myself in the familiar process of creating food my daughter will love.

I'm aware I need to pull myself together. It isn't like me to be a mess; I'm usually organised and sensible. I hate that I keep reaching for alcohol while I'm going through this and I'm aware I need to snap out of it soon. It's not good for me and I don't want Freya to pick up on what's going on.

The problem is, I'm the sort of person who always has a plan. But my world has shattered into tiny pieces and I'm not sure what I'm going to do next. All of my career goals seem trivial now and the thought of continuing to live in the house I shared with Jesse makes my skin itch. Everything is in flux. Everything is amplified. With each passing week, I'm losing my grip on more and more aspects of my life.

This winter escape is meant to be a momentary respite but I'm uncomfortable in this setting. Staying in Erin's enviable chalet, with its silk bedsheets, fancy hand soaps and enviable views, is making me feel more than a little off-kilter. And there are too many people in the resort. I thought being around more people might be good for me but

I found today's skiing session hard. I just want to shut everything out and be in a room by myself.

I place the muffins in the pre-warmed oven and turn up the heat, momentarily exhausted by my efforts. Sitting down heavily on the sofa, I realise the numbness that's been hanging over me has started to lift. Instead, I have a swirling vortex of thoughts. Thoughts that I don't want to pay attention to, that I don't want to pull me down into the darkness.

It hasn't escaped my attention that my biological father, Craig Turner, is in prison for double murder. And there are certain parallels between what I'm going through now and what my mum went through all those years ago. I have no recollections of the man himself and I only found out in my twenties that Craig and was my father. My mum's husband Simon was the person I called Daddy growing up. I grieved his death in a horrific untimely car crash when I was about the same age Freya is now.

It's starting to feel like this family is cursed. What are the odds of me then marrying someone who's also a killer? Is it me? Something to do with the Bailey women? And what does this mean for my darling daughter – is murder in her blood? Is it genetic, something we're all capable of? Or is it purely circumstantial? Is there the potential for all of us to be pushed to our limits, pushed to the edge of reason?

I can't shake this line of questioning but I don't want to be pulled down into further depths of despair with these thoughts. And so, I find myself treading the familiar path to the wooden cabinet where the alcohol is kept. My fingers tremble as I reach for the handle and pull open the door. My brain is screaming at me to stop, telling me not to do this, not to succumb to the bottle again. But the temptation for a brief respite, for oblivion to numb the pain, wins over the voice in my head that's protesting against my actions.

In one swift movement, I swipe an open bottle of red wine at the front of the cabinet. There's not much left in it, but I greedily gulp down the sweet liquid in the bottom of the glass bottle. And then the floodgates are opened. I unscrew the lid to the next bottle of wine. I don't even bother pouring this either, I just take glug after glug from the thin stem of the bottle.

It doesn't take long for the desired effects to kick in. But I've gone too far this time. My vision swirls and I stumble. I can't stop myself from falling down onto the hard wooden floor.

And the world goes white...

Chapter Ten

Leah

Escaping into the chill night air, I'm glad to be out of the house. It's been wonderful to watch a movie with the kids but I need a few hours apart from my family. I'm not used to spending so much time with them – or anyone. I've acclimatised to travelling solo, making intermittent friends and then moving on to the next place, the next group of people.

As I take a brisk walk, I feel my phone vibrating in my pocket. I've been trying to avoid screen time. I scheduled a batch of social media posts on our journey here so I wouldn't have to be online so much during this trip. I need a break, but the habitual pull of checking different platforms is strong and hard to ignore. So, automatically, I grab my phone and check the message.

It's from another anonymous number. My mouth goes dry as I read the words:

I'M CLOSER THAN YOU THINK.

I look around wildly, expecting someone to jump out onto the pathway I'm progressing along. But everything is quiet. People are either in their chalets or checking out the entertainment complex. Increasing my pace, I can see the bright lights of the various bars and restaurants ahead. I'm only about a five-minute walk away and the pathway is lit up by old-fashioned, cast-iron streetlamps that remind me of *The Chronicles of Narnia*. There are also plenty of chalets only metres away from me. Surely no one would try to attack me in such an exposed space.

My breathing hitches up a notch. I'm certain I know who the sender of these messages is. But what if I'm wrong? What if this is a new threat? Another stalker? Someone more dangerous who's worked out my whereabouts? It wouldn't be out of the realms of possibility. My life as an influencer is widely accessible online and, as a result, there are so many of my followers who feel they know me. They interact with my posts as though they're my friends. That's absolutely fine by me – I want to create genuine connections – but it becomes scary when unknown people develop obsessions. And those obsessions can develop into something far more sinister...

I'm so close to the entertainment village now, I can see people sitting at tables by the windows, laughing and joking. I shiver as I imagine the mystery sender staring down at me, watching me stumbling my way to perceived safety. As I hurtle towards The Ice Bar, panic rises in me. The message said they were close. There must be hundreds of people out for a good time tonight and the sender could be any one of them.

Arriving at the entrance, I breathlessly nod to the security staff who let me straight in. For a brief moment, I wonder if I should show the stocky man at the door the threatening message. Share the fear I might be in trouble and get his help. But I can't do that, for the same reason I haven't gone to the police over these messages in the first place.

There's no way I can risk my reputation, my successful business, my lifestyle. I draw in deep shaky breaths as I wait in the foyer of The

Ice Bar. I've got to pull myself together before I meet with Xavier. My mind has gone into overdrive but, as reason catches up with me, I wrestle my fears under control and I look at the message again.

Yes, it's from a different number but the capital letters and the brash intent is still the same as in all the other texts I've received recently. It's highly likely this isn't another random person but the same person who's been harassing me for the last few months: Lindsay.

'Hi, do you have a booking?'

I snap back to the present and take in the woman before me. She's dressed in a big silver coat, with fur around the hood.

'Um...' I stumble, trying to remember what Xavier said. My nerves are still jittery.

'She does.' Xavier appears by my side, arriving just at the right time. 'It's under Xavier Knight, for four people.'

'Right.' The Ice Bar employee checks her electronic device. 'Gotcha, step this way.'

Xavier gives me a quick hug. 'Good to see you.'

I'm pleased to see his familiar face and begin to calm as a result. I erase all thoughts of stalkers and anonymous messages from my mind and resolve to enjoy the evening as best as I can. I've had threats like these before and they've come to nothing, so I've just got to hope this time it's the same.

We file towards a cloakroom area. 'This is Fernando, you met briefly earlier on.'

We come to a stop and I flash Xavier my best smile and then nod at Fernando. He raises his hand in response and stares at me in the same way he did before. He's wearing a blue jumper with the slogan, '*Getting Piste*' written across it.

'And this is Isla.'

I give a warm hello to the athletic girl Xavier introduces but I'm instantly assessing her and wondering what her connection to Xavier is. Isla is tall and slim with brunette hair tied back in a high ponytail. She's naturally pretty, fresh-faced without any make-up on and a smattering of freckles across her upturned nose. I take note of the trendy apres-ski outfit she's wearing, comprising a multicoloured crop top, loose-fitting trousers and an over-sized white jacket which she's in the process of peeling off.

'Nice to meet you,' Isla says, her tone welcoming. 'Xavier's told me a lot about you.'

Xavier shakes his head in embarrassment.

'All good I hope?' Injecting amusement in my voice but still trying to join the dots between this trio.

'Of course! And you're that influencer, aren't you? I follow you.'

I start to answer but my words are interrupted as big silver jackets identical to those worn by the staff members are passed out to the four of us. I wrinkle my nose in response; they're not exactly the height of fashion.

Fernando laughs. 'Not your style.'

'It'll keep you warm in there,' Xavier assures me.

We shrug on the shiny silver layers and then laugh at how ridiculous we all look.

'Now this is a photo moment!' I snap a selfie of us all.

'Are you going to share that with your legions of fans?' Xavier asks.

'Not if you don't want me to,' I say as I take another photograph of just me against the backdrop of The Ice Bar sign. I've taken so many pictures that it's now just instinct for me to click away, having a feel for the right angles and the content that my followers want to see.

The door to the bar is opened and we step through. The temperature instantly plummets and I now appreciate the need for the overzealous outerwear. The expansive room is floor-to-ceiling ice. Literally everything is sculpted out of ice.

'This is amazing!' I've never seen anything like this before.

We head to the bar – also made out of ice – and I watch as the bartender pours out electric-blue liquid into several cocktail glasses. My phone is still in hand and I'm eagerly taking a succession of photos, knowing this is going to go down a storm on my socials. Everyone around us is similarly dressed in the over-sized silver coats. I needn't have spent so much time choosing my outfit, as it's completely swamped in the thick material. I'm grateful for it though, along with the warm black gloves that were given out too.

'I love your brand,' Isla tells me, and she sounds sincere.

'Thank you,' I say, feeling a little awkward about her praise. It always startles me when someone in real life comments on my work. I'm used to feedback like this in an online forum but it's always a novelty when someone makes a positive comment to my face. A little burst of pride shoots through me. I've worked so hard to get this far and it makes me even more determined not to allow anyone to try to sabotage what I've created.

'So how do you guys all know each other?' I ask, wanting to find out if Xavier is still single or if there's something going on between him and Isla.

'Fernando and I were at university together,' Xavier explains. I remember this detail from earlier and wonder if it's the same deal for Isla.

'And Isla is a ski instructor, she's been out here a few years now and she's definitely the person I have to credit for helping me to master my skis.'

'Yeah, you were like Bambi before I stepped in,' Isla teases him.

Xavier nods. 'That's fair. My mother was in despair, she'd spent years and a heap of money trying to get me to a passable level. I think she'll be forever grateful.'

There's a closeness between the two of them, and they've known each other for a while. Have I read the signs from Xavier all wrong?

'Oh, I'll have to sign up to one of your sessions,' I say. 'I'm a complete beginner.'

'I'm sure Xavier can help you out,' Fernando smirks, as he hands drinks out to all of us.

Xavier colours as he says, 'I'd be more than happy to assist.'

As the evening wears on, I begin to feel assured there isn't anything romantic between Isla and Xavier. They're behaving like great friends but there doesn't appear to be anything more to it than that. And, when we go to the bathroom – which is also in keeping with the ice theme – Isla tells me how much Xavier likes me and how he won't stop going on about me.

It feels a little teenager-ish, but it's good to have this insider information. My confidence is boosted and I go back into the bar with a renewed sense of certainty that tonight is the night when Xavier and I will finally get together properly.

As the conversation flows, I forget my troubles for a while and immerse myself in this experience. Casting my eyes around the space, I take in the enormous icicles hanging from the ceiling and the striking ice sculptures of different animals. Twisted ice pillars are lit up in multicolours and a snow machine adds to the atmosphere, scattering puffs of white into the air and giving the realistic impression of falling snow inside the building. I'm absolutely loving the setting – and loving the company even more.

Xavier throws an arm around my shoulders and I lean into him. It's been good to spend time with a group of people my age but I'm now wishing it was just the two of us. Fernando and Isla get the hint and move off to the dance floor.

Xavier and I talk for a little while longer and then he tips my head up and kisses me. Heat floods through my body, feeling even more intense in contrast to the cold room around me. Time stops still and we lose ourselves in the moment. There's no doubting it now: Xavier is just as keen as I am.

'I can't believe I'm here with you,' he whispers in my ear. 'You're beautiful.'

I blush in response and I'm about to say something in return but Isla and Fernando rejoin us. Xavier and I spring apart. Fernando's eyes are on me once more.

I glance at my watch and realise it's quite late. I'm suddenly feeling tired after the exercise this afternoon and the social interactions tonight.

My phone buzzes in my pocket and I once again reach for it. My willpower is low after a few drinks and I hope it's just a normal message from a friend. But it's not.

My eyes widen in fear. This time there's no message, just a photo.

The image is me with my head resting on Xavier's shoulder. It must've been taken about half an hour ago. Whoever is stalking me has been here, in this room. I feel the blood drain from my face and I look up sharply.

Isla is staring at me. 'Are you OK?' she asks, a look of concern crossing her face.

But is it real? Or is she feigning? I don't know her at all; could she or Fernando be behind this? They've been with us all evening, maybe one of them took the photo?

I'm jumping to conclusions but it's hard not to right now. Anyone in this room could've sent the creepy image. Standing up sharply, the world spins. Xavier is at my side steadying me.

'What's wrong?'

'I have to go,' I splutter hurriedly, looking around. No one else appears to be paying me any attention. There aren't any faces in the crowd who are looking my way. But someone is here. Someone is watching me.

I don't stop to say goodbye. I rush towards the exit, tugging the silver jacket off as I go.

'Leah, wait!' Xavier is behind me and pulls up beside me as I retrieve my things from the cloakroom. 'What happened?'

I don't even know where to start. Should I trust him with my secret? If I tell him it might scare him off, make him lose interest. So I keep quiet.

'You don't have to say anything but let me walk you back. It's late.'

I'm pretty sure Xavier has nothing to do with this, so I nod my acceptance. We walk back through a picturesque snowy scene but I can't appreciate his attentiveness. I'm on edge and just want to get back to the chalet, away from the crowd of people we've just left.

'Thank you for walking me back,' I manage to stutter. After giving Xavier a fleeting kiss on the cheek, I send him on his way. I'm aware he must think I'm rude or moody or unpredictable. I call after him, telling him I'll ring him, and he turns and starts to double back. But I can't think straight right now, so I give another wave and go inside.

I hurtle into my bedroom and make sure the door is locked. Analysing the photograph again, it's plain to see the person behind the camera was in The Ice Bar at the same time as me.

I feel dizzy at the idea they were so close. This isn't just empty threats anymore. My stalker is here in the ski resort. If they wanted to frighten me, then they've achieved that.

But what if they're planning to do more than just scare me?

And what will their next move be?

Chapter Eleven
Nadia

I enter the kitchen and immediately feel like something isn't right. A mother's instinct.

It's almost 1 a.m. and I heard Leah noisily re-enter the chalet about an hour ago. But that wasn't what got me up out of my bed. It was the faint smell of burning.

I flick the light on and observe the scene in front of me. The column of smoke pouring from the oven grabs my attention. I cross the space as quickly as I can and switch the dial on the oven to off. The stench of burning chocolate hits me full on but, thankfully, whatever is inside the oven hasn't fully caught on fire. I grab a wet dishcloth and manage to successfully extinguish the small, flickering flames dancing over the tray of food. I swiftly open the windows, receiving an icy blast of air as I throw them wide. The smoke quickly clears. Thank God I woke up when I did. If I hadn't there could've been serious consequences. I briefly wonder why the fire alarm didn't go off. Then my thoughts turn to how this fire started. My worry morphs into anger as it hits me how awful a fire could've been in this wooden chalet. I wince when I think about how fast it could've spread...

I don't have to look far to work out what happened.

On the floor, in a tangled heap of clothes, is Sasha. There are two empty spirit bottles discarded on the worktop. Sasha's crumpled figure alarms me. I bend hastily to check her over, frightened that she's inhaled a quantity of the smoke or hurt herself in some other way.

'Sasha!' She's not responding.

My hand shakes as I hold her wrist, feeling for a pulse.

I let out a breath I didn't know I was holding when I discover her heartbeat is regular and steady.

I sweep the dark mass of curls from her face and give her a firm shake. Her eyes fly open.

'Sasha, are you OK?'

She groans and tries to sit up but fails. I help to heft her from the floor and guide her towards the sofa. She looks a complete mess but I'm reassured that, beyond being wasted, she's not otherwise hurt.

Leaving her to wake up properly, I swipe the bottles into the recycling bin and slowly open the oven. Faint wisps of smoke are still curling from the mouth of the open oven. Removing the cloth, I find rows of muffins all burnt to a cinder. Shaking my head, I fill a glass of cold water for Sasha and return to her side.

My eldest daughter takes the drink from me and, as she does, I notice her teeth are chattering from the cool air coming in through the windows. I set about closing them up again and then sit down next to Sasha. There's no point in admonishing her; even though I'm finding it difficult to hold back on what I really think, she's in no fit state to go over the situation.

Instead, I take her hand and, as I do, she bursts into tears.

'Sasha...' My heart breaks for her. I let her cry it out, smoothing her hair like I used to do when she was a child. We stay like that for a while and then her sobs eventually subside.

'Come on, let's get you to bed.' I lead her to the bedroom we're sharing and we find that Freya has crept into the single bed allocated to Sasha. Sasha gives a small smile and slithers in next to her own daughter.

'Sleep well,' I say softly.

I try to get some rest myself but end up tossing and turning. I'm surprised Leah didn't notice Sasha or notice that the oven was switched on but it sounded as though she dashed straight through the door and into her room when she returned to the chalet earlier, so I'm guessing she didn't pause to go into the open-plan room. And I suspect the smoke had only just started billowing when I entered the communal space. I think again how lucky it was I was awake and able to diffuse things.

There's absolutely no way I'm getting any proper sleep, so at 5.30 a.m. I'm up and getting myself ready. I allow myself a leisurely soak in the generously proportioned bath and then spend time applying my make-up in front of the bathroom mirror. Leah has given me some good hair and beauty tips in recent years and, thanks to her, I manage to make myself look a little bit more youthful as a result.

Next, I bustle around in the kitchen. Tidying away the remains of Sasha's disastrous attempts at baking and then concentrating on making the room birthday-ready for Freya. It's hard to believe my little granddaughter is turning ten. I remember how proud I was when I saw her small, scrunched-up baby face for the very first time. She's brought me so much joy over the years. She's such a breath of fresh air and a kind-hearted soul as well. Today should be special for her. I know she will be missing Jesse so I want to create as many happy diversions as I can. Starting with balloons.

I packed a stash of pink balloons in my suitcase and I set to work on blowing every one of them up. I'm out of breath when I finish but satisfied that Freya will be delighted by how many of the balloons I've been able to inflate. I string them all up around the room and then busy myself with hanging up birthday banners as well. I've even remembered the plastic pink tablecloth that's been used many times for Freya and my daughters before her. I've always looked after my belongings well, partly out of frugality, and as a result they've tended to last. It's lovely to be able to reuse items that have so many memories attached to them.

The rest of the house begins waking up. Erin is the first to join me.

'Gosh,' she says, looking round at the now very pink space. 'You've transformed the place.'

'I hope you don't mind,' I say, unsure if I might've overstepped the mark as it dawns on me how particular Erin is about the decor in her properties.

'No, no,' Erin insists with a wave of her hand. 'It's for the birthday girl.'

As she says this, Freya herself skips into the room singing, 'Happy birthday to me!'

She stops short and claps her hands in glee. 'Nana!' she exclaims, 'did you do all this for me?' Her little eyes are as wide as saucers as she takes in the banners and balloons.

My heart squeezes at her response and her face lights up in just the way I'd hoped.

The other two children join us and they're suitably excited too. I sit the three of them at the very pink table and serve up some breakfast waffles.

Next to each other, both with their red hair tied back in fluorescent-coloured scrunchies, Freya and Ophelia look even more like each other than usual. Given the closeness in age and the similarity in their complexions and colourings, Freya could easily be mistaken for a sibling to the twins. They're so alike it wouldn't be a stretch of the imagination for a stranger to assume the three of them are triplets.

Leah drifts in to join us next. She looks a little pale but I put it down to her having a late night.

'Did you have a good time?' I ask her.

She nods but doesn't look enthused. I don't press her for the details just yet, but usually if she's been out on a date that's gone well she's sparkling the next day. Her behaviour suggests that perhaps the evening didn't go as intended. Maybe Xavier's already out of the picture and therefore I won't have to conjure up ways to keep Leah away from him.

'And how was your day yesterday Erin?' I'm determined to find out if she really went skiing because it didn't look as though she'd exerted herself at all when she joined us yesterday afternoon.

But Erin doesn't respond to my question. Instead, she says, 'What's this?' And points at the charred muffins in the bin.

My hand flies to my mouth. As no damage was done, I wasn't going to bring up the burnt food unless I absolutely had to.

Erin is looking at me with her eyebrows raised.

'Nothing to worry about,' I say as casually as I can. 'Just a few overdone cakes.'

'Overdone? These have been burnt to ashes.' Erin's face is stern and I realise I need to come clean.

'Sasha was making muffins for Freya's birthday, they just ended up in the oven a bit too long... It's OK, I sorted it.'

'Can I open my presents?' Freya cuts in, itching to unwrap the small pile of parcels, all in pink wrapping paper.

I pounce on her interruption and turn away from Erin's questioning gaze. 'Let's wait until Mummy joins us,' I reply.

'Why is Mummy not up?' Freya's mouth is a little downturned.

I check the clock and realise it's 10 a.m. already. 'She's tired, my love.'

I can't help feeling annoyed. It's Freya's birthday and Sasha shouldn't have gotten herself into such a state last night. I'm about to go and wake her when the door swings open.

'Mummy!' Freya runs to Sasha and throws her arms around her waist.

'Happy birthday sweetheart,' Sasha says weakly.

Freya drags Sasha straight towards the presents, eager to get started. Within seconds, wrapping paper is being shredded to pieces. Freya unveils a new Barbie doll and a skipping rope. We couldn't bring too much because of the luggage allowance, so her presents this year were chosen based on size and weight.

'Slow down!' I chuckle.

'Yeah, I won't be able to get any photos at the rate you're going!' Leah laughs.

'Here's my present.' Erin interjects, handing Freya a small, pink envelope.

By the look that passes over my granddaughter's face, I can see she's wondering if there's anything of excitement in the envelope. Freya opens this a little more slowly and, to her credit, stops to admire the unicorn on the front of the card.

A piece of paper flutters out and Freya picks it up, slowly reading the contents to herself. And then she springs up and flings herself at Erin.

'Auntie Erin! This is what I always wanted!'

'I thought you might like it,' Erin gushes.

'Tickets to see *Matilda*!' Freya dances around the room. 'For all of us!'

'That's very generous,' I say to Erin.

A lump forms in my throat. It was ultimately Erin's choice not to be in contact with the rest of the family over the last decade, but I can't help feeling responsible for her not wanting to see us. I'm just so delighted that my family are together again and that Erin is making an effort.

'I thought it would be fun.' She smiles at Freya and Ophelia, who are both bouncing up and down on their heels with elation.

Sasha hasn't said anything. She's remained stony-faced and detached.

'Here,' Leah furnishes Sasha with a large mug of coffee.

I cross my fingers that a hit of caffeine is what Sasha needs to right herself.

Freya is brimming with happiness as she returns to open the rest of her presents. She receives so many thoughtful items: nail varnish and a nail stamp kit from Leah, books from me, a charm bracelet from Sasha.

'I love being ten!' Freya enthuses.

It's sweet to see her so enamoured with her gifts.

'I think it's birthday cake time!'

My words are greeted with cheers from the children. But before I can say anything more, Sasha stands up abruptly. She looks grey.

In the next second, she's darting in the direction of the bathroom. I sigh. She's in no fit state for a ten-year-old's birthday. Freya's lip trembles: she may only be young but she realises something isn't right with her mother.

'Change of plan,' I breeze, as though nothing's the matter. 'Let's go and make a snowman first!'

This suggestion is probably the best distraction I could've come up with. There's a flurry of activity as woolly hats and colourful scarves are put on, along with welly boots and warm coats.

'I'm going to make the biggest snowball you've ever seen!' Jasper shouts at the top of his voice.

'And I'm going to make a snow queen,' Ophelia chimes in.

We're all heading out the door in five minutes flat. It's amazing how fast children can go when they really want to. A complete contrast to how long it takes for them to get out the door on a school morning.

Leah and Erin join in the fun as well. Soon we're all absorbed in the task of packing handfuls of snow to form snow people. The children are adding lots of creativity to the task at hand, gathering various materials for buttons, eyes and arms. It's brilliant to see my children and grandchildren together like this, with the majestic mountains in the background and the village of charming wooden chalets as a backdrop, but I'm acutely aware that Sasha isn't with us. She's alone inside and I do feel a bit guilty for being out here with everyone else. I suspect she might just want some space to attempt to straighten herself out.

We end up with three very different snow statues. A snow queen made by Ophelia and Leah, a very traditional snowman made by me and Jasper, and a snow dog made by Freya and Erin. Leah, true to form, takes lots of pictures of us all with our snow creations.

'This is sooooooo awesome!' a little voice says as we're gathering up our things.

I turn to my left, expecting to see Freya. Instead, it's Ophelia and she's now clapping her hands and singing, 'Happy birthday to me' in a voice that sounds strangely like Freya's.

Leah is laughing hard. 'Ophelia, where did you learn to do that?'

Ophelia continues to impersonate Freya and is eerily accurate.

'Ophelia, you're too good!' Leah is laughing. 'You're an actress in the making!'

I must admit, she is convincing but I have no idea why Ophelia is mimicking Freya. And, judging by the look on Freya's face, she's quite upset about it. Her eyes are welling up with tears but both Ophelia and Leah are oblivious to this.

'Freya.' I draw my granddaughter close to me. 'It's OK,' I whisper.

'Do I really sound like that?'

'You sound like you, just lovely.' I usher Freya indoors as I hear Erin telling Ophelia to stop. I can't help but feel protective over Freya. She's the granddaughter I've known from birth and I feel a little appalled at Ophelia's behaviour. I'm concerned she was being deliberately unkind. Perhaps that's not the case and I'm overthinking things but, despite Ophelia's knack for impersonation, I'm not impressed with what she just did.

Fleetingly, it occurs to me that Ophelia wanted to make Freya sad on her birthday because she's jealous of Freya being the centre of attention. In the short time I've known Ophelia, it's become apparent that she likes to have all eyes on her. If that's so, then it's probably just a case of children being children. However, the alternative could be that Ophelia is wanting to torment Freya as a result of their clash the previous day. That would be much more worrying...

As we troop back inside, I hurriedly shake off my outer layers and go in search of my eldest daughter. I discover Sasha back in her room, passed out on her bed. Placing my hands on my hips, I let out a ragged breath. I know Sasha is struggling but I thought she'd try to keep things together on Freya's birthday. Freya means the world to her, so the fact she hasn't been able to get through today – not even the start of it – is a huge cause for alarm. I'm starting to think this holiday wasn't the best plan after all. Maybe we all need to deal with our issues head on, rather than putting the inevitable on hold.

If things don't improve, I'm going to cut the trip short and take Sasha home. I'm probably just being paranoid, but I can't shake the feeling that something bad is going to happen to her.

Chapter Twelve

Erin

I'm so angry with Sasha and my mother. It's obvious Sasha nearly started a fire with those muffins - I dread to think what happened. But what makes it worse is that our mother was covering for her. If I hadn't opened the bin when I did, I may never have found out about it. I'm guessing that was the intention, for my mother to quietly sweep things away and pretend like it never happened. A burst of rage shoots through me and I clench my jaw tightly. If she's been untruthful about this, what else might my mother be hiding?

I pass out bowls of sweets to the children, partly as a birthday treat and partly to keep them occupied for a bit so I can grab five minutes' peace. I make a green tea for myself and then sit in the chair next to the expansive window. In the distance, I can see the dark shapes of skiers weaving like a line of ants against the pure white snow. I long to be out on the mountains myself, to lose myself in the freedom of being on the slopes. But my mother was insistent that we stay here today, to celebrate Freya's birthday together. And just look how that's turning out...

I briefly close my eyes and listen to the chatter of the children in the background. I'm having flashbacks of growing up in a household with two siblings. Sometimes we were all the best of friends and sometimes we hated each other. There were constant shifts in allegiances depending on our ages, moods or even just the day of the week. Somehow Sasha's faults used to be sheltered in exactly the same way her mistake has been today, while Leah used to get away with practically anything. However, when it was my turn to screw up, my mother used to take a very different approach. She was obsessed with me being the 'naughty one' and that obsession eventually shaped my reality. I decided that if I was always being called out for doing the wrong thing, then I may as well break a few rules along the way. That attitude has sometimes served me well, and at other times has landed me in serious hot water. Ultimately, it led me to becoming the person I am today: a wealthy woman with blood on her hands.

I've taken plenty of risks in my time, so it wasn't a huge leap for me to take another one. The truth is, I knew Sasha was going to be worse for wear today. How? Because I planned it. I knew there was no way that she'd get through one evening without reaching for an alcoholic drink. I've been observing her over the last few weeks and her issues with consuming too much have been easy to spot. So last night I gave the two wine bottles in the drinks cabinet an extra kick. I spiked the wine and then made sure the bottles were at the front of the cabinet. I knew only Sasha would reach for them. I didn't spike them too heavily of course, but just enough to ensure it would have a negative effect. And, if Sasha chose to drink more than her fill, that's not my fault.

One thing I hadn't banked on was my sister deciding to bake muffins late in the evening. I had no idea that she was going to be responsible for a hot oven at the time she drank the alcohol, otherwise I would never have tampered with the wine. I hate to think what might have happened if my mum hadn't intervened.

The doorbell rings and I see Leah almost jump out of her seat at the sound. I stride to the front door and open it. We're not expecting any visitors but I can guess who it is.

'Erin, hello dear! How are you?'

Marnie O'Connor owns the chalet across the way from us. She's a firm fixture in the ski resort and someone I've come to think of as a friend as well as a neighbour over the years. However, I'm not keen on her coming in when Sasha could emerge in any kind of state at any minute, so I resolve to have a quick chat and send her on her way today rather than inviting her inside.

Marnie asks how the children are and then – the inevitable – she asks me how I'm finding being at the chalet without Aaron. I know that I just have to square my shoulders and get through these kinds of conversations but it's not easy. Looking down, I twist my wedding band round my finger. It's an instinctive reaction now anytime Aaron's name is mentioned. It means I avoid eye contact with the person talking to me and I find the act of doing this gives me something physical to focus on, which helps to take me out of the situation a little.

'He will be missed by everyone...' Marnie is continuing, not picking up on how awkward my body posture is.

I just want to embrace my new life now that I'm free from Aaron's control. But not a day goes past without his name being mentioned. It's still only a short time since his death so it's to be expected but I'm finding it difficult to live out such a big secret day by day. I've thought about selling everything and starting from scratch somewhere new. It's an option but I don't really want to uproot my children from their lives and I'm determined to continue to make the hotel a success. I've put so many hours and so much energy into the business, it would be hard to walk away. In the coming months, I'm sure the mentions of my husband and the pitiful looks on people's faces will slowly fade. If not, I will have to reassess my plans.

'It's so cold out here.' Marnie rubs her hands together, the older woman hinting in a not-so-subtle way that she wants to be invited in.

'It's absolutely freezing!' I agree. 'I'd better go, Marnie, I need to get back to the children, but let's catch up again soon.'

Marnie's face falls slightly but she doesn't press me further. I watch as she crosses the path back to her own chalet, where she resides by herself. She's a short woman with lots of energy and a zest for the slopes that's not easily matched, even by people half her age. She's been a useful ally at times, so I need to make sure I keep in her good books.

Before I turn to go inside, I see there's a disturbed section in the snow to the left of our chalet. I pull my boots on and fling a coat around me. Digging my nails into the palms of my hands, I walk a few paces to where the smooth snow has been messed with. It could just be a section where someone has slipped when walking off the main path but my gut instinct tells me it's more than that. And I'm right.

There in the white blanket of snow is another message. Is this meant for me? Should I be worried? I lay my palm flat and blur the snow together, erasing the letters so they're no longer there for anyone else to see. But the words are imprinted on my brain.

I KNOW WHAT YOU DID.

Chapter Thirteen

Sasha

Lying on a soft bed with a panoramic view of the snow-topped mountains, I feel stressed and wound up. The luxurious surroundings of the spa aren't having any impact on my mood. I'm trying so hard to allow myself to de-stress but my muscles are taut and adrenaline courses through my body. In my mind, I go over and over my daughter's birthday. Yesterday was a complete failure. I feel absolutely mortified that I was so hungover I couldn't even join in to watch Freya blow out her candles, let alone eat a piece of the sweetly iced birthday cake. I wanted my daughter to have the perfect tenth birthday, but I ruined it with my behaviour. I've got a lot of making up to do – to Freya, to my mum and to Erin. Because Erin found out about the burnt muffins. I can understand why she's so furious. It was totally irresponsible of me and I could've put all our lives in danger. It was lucky Mum came to check things when she did.

Once more, I try to move my thoughts on to something else. However, there are two things I just don't get. One: why wasn't the fire alarm working? Mum told me yesterday evening, when she was rightly giving me the third degree, that a quantity of smoke was already billowing out of the oven when she walked into the kitchen. And when she checked, the fire alarm was emitting a small, pathetic beep that no one would've heard. I'm surprised Erin hadn't got this tested as part of the preparations for us arriving. She thought of everything, so it's odd this vital check wasn't done. Then again, she's had a lot going on lately.

The second thing that's been bothering me is that I know I had a few slugs of alcohol – and that's on me. But it wasn't a significant amount in comparison to the way I've been drinking in the last few weeks. So I find it strange it affected me so much. Perhaps it was a combination of tiredness as well as drink that made me crash out on the hard kitchen floor. I wish it hadn't happened though, and this is my wake-up call. I need to get things under control, otherwise it's going to impact Freya.

I shift position and lie on my front, cupping my face in my hands and trying to concentrate on the view of ice and snow. My mum booked the spa as a treat for us all this morning. There's a children's area where they can do yoga, quiet drawing and eat healthy snacks while the adults spend a few hours in the heated outdoor pool over-looking the mountains or indulging in a deep-muscle massage or even spending some time in the salt grotto. There's so many choices for different types of mind, body and soul relaxation that, honestly, I found the options quite overwhelming when the list of treatments were presented to me.

Instead of using the sauna or steam baths, I've decided to lie on a simple spa bed that feels as though it's part of the mountain scenery. But, after half an hour, there's no sign of the tranquil scenery soothing me in any way, shape or form. So I swing my legs off the bed and make my way to the indoor pool area. Maybe some gentle exercise will do me good. As I step down into the clear water, the warmth immediately envelops me. I exhale slowly, letting go of some of my tension, before finding a spot in the corner of the expansive pool to rest while I get my bearings.

Looking around me, I take in the tall, vaulted glass ceiling and stare up at the soft, blue sky above. Everything about this spa has been designed to make a person feel part of the snowy mountain setting. Finally, I begin to feel a little calmer. The warm water is like a gentle balm and I watch other people chatting or swimming around me. On the other side of the pool, I spot Leah. She's zooming up and down her swim lane at a steady speed, completely immersed in what she's doing. Erin and my mum booked in for facials and full-body massages so I'm sure I won't be seeing them for a while. Perhaps I should've joined them, but it's too late now and there's plenty of other things I can do.

I half-heartedly swim one length and, when I reach the end, I catch sight of a Jacuzzi tucked away in the corner of the room. It's empty and the idea of the bubbles appeals to me. So I transfer myself out of the pool and into the inviting frothy water. Locating the correct button, I switch the jets on and settle myself into a seat. This is exactly what I needed. My aching body gradually begins to loosen and I give myself up to the blissful feeling of being in the water.

As I lean back, I resolve to straighten myself out and commit to a fresh start. After all, that's what this winter escape is meant to be about. Erin, despite the animosity between us, still asked me and Freya to come on this family getaway – she even paid for our flights. She didn't have to do that. We hadn't spoken for ten years and, as I recently discovered, part of that was to do with my husband Jesse being secretly infatuated with her. And, if that wasn't damaging enough for our relationship, Jesse went and stunned us all by killing Erin's husband Aaron in a drunken altercation which resulted in Aaron plunging from the top of their marble staircase to his death.

Taking a deep breath, I imagine things from Erin's perspective. She's just lost her husband, she's now a single parent to twins, and all of her hopes, dreams and plans have also been turned on their head. With Jesse now in prison, our situations are similar. We're both learning to navigate a new reality as single mothers as well as coming to terms with what happened.

I'm not sure, in her shoes, if I would have extended an olive branch to the wife of my husband's killer in the way she has to me. I'm in awe of how she's keeping things together so well. I've felt so isolated in the last few bleak weeks, which have felt like they've stretched on for an eternity. Erin is probably one of the few people who can understand what I'm going through. This new acknowledgement of my sister's situation makes me see things a bit differently. No wonder she's furious with me for my drunken behaviour and almost causing a fire. She's been trying her best and I'm ashamed to admit that I've been churlish in return. I guess I'm still feeling quite wary of her. She looks exactly like the sister I remember but, after a whole decade of not being in each other's lives, there are so many things I don't know about her and so much that is different.

As the water swirls around me, I also remember her gift to Freya – tickets to the theatre. Erin has been lovely to Freya and this generous gesture is just one example of that. This brief moment of respite has given me the opportunity to reassess things. I've got some bridges to mend and plenty of making up to do. So I'm going to dig deep and muster as much willpower as I can to curb the excessive drinking habit

I've developed. And I'm going to make the effort to be a better mother, daughter and sister.

Outside, I can see a group of skiers having a lesson. They're walking sideways up the mountain, lifting one leg and then the other. With their dark helmets and dark goggles against fluorescent ski wear they do look rather comical. I watch one figure stumble and then pick themselves up again, still smiling. I've lost my confidence in the last month, even in my ability to do a physical activity like skiing. But, watching this ski lesson from my vantage point in the Jacuzzi, I realise that it doesn't matter how well I'm mastering the skis. What matters is enjoying the experience – and picking myself up and going again.

Glancing around the space, I see the pool area has emptied out quite a bit. It must be coming up to lunchtime already. I need to get myself out and find the others, but I'm finally feeling composed and peaceful in a way that I haven't done for such a long time. My eyes are heavy, and I struggle to blink away the tiredness, a wave of exhaustion suddenly overcoming me.

I give into it. And I sink backwards into the bubbles, into the froth, into the water...

Chapter Fourteen

Leah

'What's going on?' I cry, rushing towards the commotion.

Swiping water from my eyes, my vision clears but the scene before me stays the same. I thought I was seeing things, but no, this is really happening.

On the tiled floor of the indoor pool area a woman is on all fours and two lifeguards are with her. One speaking loudly into a crackling walkie-talkie and the other slapping the woman on the back while she coughs up water.

Alarmed, I propel myself forward. 'Is she OK? Will she be all right?' I squawk as I throw myself to my knees to see for myself.

My eldest sister is spluttering and her face is bright red. The lifeguard gives Sasha another firm slap on the back and she spits up an impressive amount of water. Rocking back on her heels, Sasha then takes in a huge lungful of air. And then another. And another.

'Do you know this person?' the lifeguard who's been speaking into the walkie-talkie asks me.

'Yes, she's my sister,' I say, as I loop an arm around Sasha's shoulders. She's shivering violently.

'We found her in the Jacuzzi, she'd slipped under the water.'

I gasp sharply as I process this information. Sasha's behaviour is becoming more erratic and dangerous – the drinking, the oven incident yesterday, and now this.

'Thank you so much for helping her,' I stutter gratefully.

Another member of staff hastens towards us and drapes a thick, white towel around Sasha.

'We'd better get her checked over properly,' the new addition to our group instructs.

I assist Sasha to her feet. The redness has drained out of her face and she now looks very pale. She hasn't said a thing, appearing to be dazed.

As I guide her into a side room, I take another fluffy white towel from a stack on the shelf and use it to wrap up her long, wet hair, twisting it onto the top of her head. A member of the medical team checks her over very thoroughly.

'What happened?' I ask my sister, failing to understand how she could've got into difficulties in a Jacuzzi.

'I fell asleep,' Sasha mumbles, her head down.

'She's in shock, but otherwise fine.' I'm asked to sign an accident book, so I scrawl our names and contact information next to the column detailing the incident. The matter-of-fact woman looks at me for a beat and then says, 'Be in touch if you have any concerns.'

I thank the spa team profusely for their help as they tell us to stay in the little room for as long as needed. One of the lifeguards hands us both some very sweet tea and then they leave the two of us on our own.

As we're sitting in the small, airless room I realise Sasha has an underlying smell of alcohol about her and I cringe to think the spa team probably picked up on this too. Sasha is quietly sipping her tea;

she's still not said a word. How has my organised, successful big sister been reduced to this? And how do I help to get the real Sasha back again?

After another twenty minutes, I take Sasha back to the changing rooms; she's leaning on me for support. Together we dress and I encourage her to get ready so we can go and get some lunch, hoping that will help to restore her. I'm half expecting her to burst into tears or give some kind of reaction to her incident in the water, but she remains blank-faced.

We make our way towards the spa restaurant and, just before we enter, Sasha puts her hand on my arm.

'Leah,' her eyes are pleading. 'Please don't mention this to anyone else.'

My eyebrows shoot up. I wasn't expecting her to ask me to keep this a secret. There have been far too many truths hidden and lies covered up in this family. My instinct is to tell her no, that we at least have to share this with our mother so she's aware. But Sasha looks so broken, so desperate, that I find myself promising that I won't divulge a thing.

'Just don't do anything like that again though, what were you thinking?'

'Honestly, I was so chilled I just drifted off...'

I'm sure the effects of alcohol may have had more of an influence than she's admitting to me – or to herself.

'We've got to get things sorted for you. I want to help.'

Sasha gives me a weak smile and she looks grateful. I decide I will keep my promise to her, but only if things start to improve. If she continues to behave erratically then I will have to share this information with Mom and Erin.

We find a spot at the far end of the room and then both help ourselves to the ultra-healthy buffet. I wasn't expecting Sasha to be able to stomach anything but she acting as though she's ravenously hungry. Her plate is piled high with fancy fruit and veg. Once I've filled up my plate, we sit back down and I spread beetroot butter over my seeded bread and top it with avocado. I whip my phone out and take a photo, and then enjoy my first delicious bite.

Sasha is tucking into butternut squash and feta salad as though she hasn't just been through a traumatic experience. Maybe I'm worrying too much about it but she still hasn't said how she managed to almost drown herself in a Jacuzzi. The need to understand my sister, in order to help, pushes me to quiz her again.

'How did you end up under the water?' I gently ask her.

Sasha doesn't look at me. 'I... I was tired. Like I said, I fell asleep.'

I stare at her. I have no idea if she's telling me the truth or not. She still doesn't look up.

'Are you sure?'

She nods curtly.

'You didn't... when you started slipping under, you didn't realise?'

'I don't want to talk about it,' Sasha snaps at me. She meets my gaze now with a defiant look in her eyes.

I don't press her any further.

We eat for a few more minutes in complete silence and then I see Mom and Erin enter the room.

'Over here!' I wave to them.

They join us at the window table. I pour out glasses of lemon water for them both.

'How was your morning?' Mom asks. 'Feeling relaxed?'

My stomach flips. 'I had a great swim in the indoor pool,' I reply, because this is true. I was having a nice time before Sasha's incident.

'And the two of us have spent some time together,' I continue, as this is also true.

Sasha straightens up. 'The views are amazing,' she says. 'How was your massage?'

Mom waxes lyrical about how divine her massage was and jokes about how youthful she's going to look after her pricey facial. Erin is equally positive about her time at the spa.

Feeling deceitful for not sharing what happened to Sasha, I move the conversation on to our plans for this afternoon.

'I've booked a surprise,' Mom tells us. 'For the whole family.'

I'm not sure surprises are what any of us need right now, but I hold onto the idea that it's bound to be something that we're all going to like.

I make a game of guessing what it might be and pressing Mom for more information, which she revels in, but she keeps her cards close and doesn't unveil what this afternoon's activity is.

'We need to collect the children and then all will be revealed,' she beams, pleased with herself.

Dipping my hand in my bag, I rummage around in search of my make-up bag. I need to dab at least a bit of tinted moisturiser on my face and apply some lip gloss. I'm not used to being in public without my face made up and, occasionally, I'm recognised by a social media follower and I don't want to get caught out completely devoid of make-up.

My fingers don't alight on it though, which is strange as it's a sizeable bag.

'Hmmm...' I place my large Michael Kors handbag on the table and search more thoroughly but I still can't find it.

Frowning, I begin emptying the contents of the bag out onto the table.

'What've you lost?' Mom enquires, as she takes a mouthful of grapefruit.

'My cosmetics...'

It's ridiculous, but I feel a bit panicky. For starters, the contents contain hundreds of pounds' worth of make-up and, even more importantly, it's a collection that very specifically works for my skin. I've carefully built up the perfect complement of eyeliner, primer, foundation, highlighter, blusher and mascara and I use them multiple times a day. If I've lost my treasure trove of cosmetics then I only have a few select pieces of back-up in my suitcase. There are some shops here but a lot of the brands I use are Australian so it's unlikely I'm going to be able to replace the items easily while I'm at the ski resort.

'It's definitely not here,' I sigh in frustration.

'Did you leave it in your locker by the pool?' Sasha suggests.

'No, I put it in my handbag this morning.' I whizz back through the events of the last few hours. I didn't go to retrieve my handbag from my locker until after things had calmed down with Sasha. I'm certain that I put the cosmetics in my handbag this morning, like I always do, and I haven't used them at any point since we've been at the spa, but I guess I'm going to have to retrace my steps just to be sure. The other explanation is that I've left it back at the chalet, but I can see myself picking it up this morning. I go through a mental checklist before I go out anywhere. I know I wouldn't have left it behind.

'I'll ask at the spa reception, see if anyone has handed it in.' Mom gets up to do just this.

'No, no. Thanks but I've finished my food now. I'll go.'

'OK, meet back in the lobby area in fifteen minutes,' Mom instructs, anxious for me to be on time for whatever she has in store later on.

Making my way through the restaurant, which has suddenly filled with people, my mind is on the missing cosmetics. But then I see something that sucks the air out of me. I stop dead in my tracks.

Just metres from me, sitting at one of the tables, is her: the face behind the blackmailing over the last few months, the person who's been persistent in her pursuit of me. It's obvious now that she was also behind the most recent anonymous messages. It's Lindsay.

I almost trip over in disbelief, but my hand shoots out to steady myself and I manage to clutch onto the back of an empty chair. I blink rapidly, wondering if I'm seeing things, or if this woman is just someone who looks very similar to my stalker. There's no doubt about it though: Lindsay's fair locks cascade down her back in loose waves and she's staring straight at me. But I realise that's not all. I get goosebumps when I see who's sitting next to her. It's Lindsay's husband, Shane. He's here with her. He's the reason the hassle with Lindsay began in the first place.

I thought Lindsay was bluffing. So I'm blindsided to see them both here in person. I assumed their threats were empty ones, but now I'm seeing them in the flesh I'm not so sure.

Lindsay's unpredictable behaviour and doggedness unnerves me. This has been going on for too long now. As I remember Shane's almond-shaped eyes and floppy, golden hair I bitterly regret hooking up with him. It's been one of my biggest mistakes to date. But I truthfully had no idea that he was married. He was a regular at the beach bar that I used to hang out at. A classic, hunky Australian surfer. There was no ring on his finger and no mention of a wife. He spent weeks flirting with me. And then one warm evening we ended up kissing at sunset.

Things moved quickly from that first kiss. I was swept up by his spontaneity. At no point did Shane mention a marriage – or even an estranged partner. It was someone else at the beach bar who finally informed me that Shane was two-timing me. I remember feeling crushed, because I thought we had something special, the beginning of a relationship, it wasn't just a fling for me. It had been so much more.

Lindsay raises one hand in greeting, as if we're old friends, but I note that her eyes narrow as she does this. I could just go over there and confront them, ask them what they think they're playing at showing up here. Glancing around the full room, I curse under my breath because I can't risk a showdown in front of all these people. And Lindsay knows it. So I turn on my heel and head for the door, my heart banging loudly and blood whooshing in my ears. I'm furious the pair of them are taking things this far. They're crazy...

Anger flares in my belly as I leave the room, just as it did when I discovered the truth about Shane. I was furious that he tricked me into thinking he was single and duped me into falling for him. I remember calling him, ready to give him a piece of my mind. He didn't answer the phone though, Lindsay did. She shouted abuse at me and swore I'd pay for sleeping with her husband. I tried to explain, but she was having none of it and soon put the phone down on me. I was blistering with emotions but, naively, I thought that would be it. I wouldn't see Shane again.

I was mistaken.

Lindsay wanted to take her pain out on me. She blamed me for Shane's actions and the damage it wrought on her marriage. She sent so many messages and called me repeatedly. I kept blocking the numbers she was using, but she'd then come at me with a different caller ID. This went on for months and, in a moment of weakness, I screamed down the phone at her, asking what exactly it was that she wanted from me.

Her answer was immediate: money.

I wish I had just reported her then but I agreed. I just wanted her off my back, so I arranged for a sum to be transferred to her. It was meant to pay her off, stop her contacting me, but it did the opposite. Lindsay saw me as her new source of income and, as soon as the first payment landed in her account, she was hounding me for more. Her messages were pure blackmail: she threatened to expose my relationship with Shane online. She said she would ruin my reputation. I'd never had to deal with anything like this before – I didn't even tell my manager because I was too worried about how potentially damaging it could be. You read about these situations all the time, of sensible people tricked into parting with their hard-earned cash. And you never think it's going to happen to you.

My stomach is in knots as I remember that I just wanted Lindsay and Shane to leave my life for good so I gave in to Lindsay's financial demands. Naively, I trusted them to keep their end of the agreement and to stop hassling me. But Lindsay became bolder and greedier, eventually extracting an even bigger sum from my bank account.

My trip back to England was an opportunity for me to put distance between me and the couple trying to ruin me. On the other side of the world, I thought I'd shake them off. No such luck. Lindsay's threats have become more unhinged and Shane has been supporting his wife in her endeavours to prise more money from me. Following me halfway across the globe is another level though and it shows me just how dangerous they might be.

I exhale a shaky breath. What am I going to do?

Going to the police is an option and has always been an option. I didn't want to get them involved for a number of reasons though. Lindsay has played me well, because she knows how valuable my reputation is to me. It's the basis of my entire influencer business and if dented could threaten my future success. After I made the first payment, it occurred to me I'd made a massive error not just because of the loss of money but because I'm not keen for the police to start scrutinising my finances…

I'm only human though and I panicked when Lindsay came after me.

Just like I'm panicking now.

Checking back over my shoulder as I stride down the corridor, the two of them must still be sitting at their table because there's no sign of them coming after me. Temporary relief washes over me but I know this doesn't mean they're not going to hunt me down at some point on this holiday. I recall the feeling of being watched as I made my way to The Ice Bar and the photo I received of me and Xavier. I'm sure Lindsay and Shane must be behind both of those things.

The question is, why are they at the ski resort? And what do they want from me next?

Chapter Fifteen

Nadia

The scene before me is just magical. Two magnificent white horses are pulling a cherry-red sleigh towards us. The three children in their bobble hats bounce up and down with excitement. It's just the reaction I was aiming for.

'We're going on a sleigh ride!' I smile widely at my family. They all look pleased at the prospect and my grandchildren cheer in delight.

Leah has already got to work on taking photos and videos. I wish she'd have just a day without the device in her hand but I understand why she's so glued to it. Apart from her generation's obsession with social media, her career as an influencer is earning her a living. Still, I dislike that she's always working and, unlike with a more traditional job, she isn't able to switch off from what she's doing.

'Thanks Mum,' Sasha says to me. 'This is just fantastic.'

I draw her in for a hug, my mind again leaping to the dangerous situation she put herself in yesterday. 'It's something a bit different, isn't it?'

'Yes, I'm sure we'll all remember this for years to come.' Sasha smiles as Freya clambers up onto the sleigh first and poses for Leah's camera.

'And if we don't, Leah will have plenty of photographs,' I joke.

Soon we're all settled in the sleigh and cosy blankets have been placed over our knees. Leah snaps a group image and then the horses are away. I relish the icy rush of air in my face and my hair, it sharpens my senses and makes me feel more alert. The scenery slides past us as the horses pick up pace. This truly is a spellbinding setting. The sky is fresh, a vast and infinite blue, and the mountains rise around us. The wooden chalets are all so quaint, clustered together against the pure white snow. I almost have to pinch myself as it's like I'm in some kind of fairytale village.

Before we left for this holiday, I spent several evenings browsing the ski resort website. I was amazed to see so many facilities out here and so many activities available. I booked up the sleigh ride immediately. The children had a tough Christmas so we kept things low-key and quiet in the initial wake of Aaron's death. I wanted to arrange something for them to make up for some of the festivities they missed out on in December. The sleigh ride fitted the bill perfectly.

There were plenty of other things that caught my eye on the website as well. I'm keen to explore the rest of the resort in more detail and I plan to book a stargazing experience in an igloo for us all next. Jasper is keen to go tobogganing and Erin has mentioned there's a picturesque walk that goes past a frozen waterfall. I want to do everything I can to fill this trip with precious memories and ensure that everyone has a good time.

As the sleigh bumps along, my daughters and grandchildren chatter animatedly, pointing out things in the landscape around them. It gives me hope that everything is going to be OK. All I want is for the shockwaves of the Christmas party to fade and a future for my children, and their children, that's filled with love and happiness.

I pull the blanket up around me a little more. Despite my big coat, warm hat and gloves and the protective roof arched above the sleigh, I'm still feeling a little chilly. The horses are directed back along the route we've just been along and the scenery on the return stretch is even more impressive. We whizz past snow-laden trees and the resort is lit up, glittering against the deep purples and blues of the sunset.

Sasha is sitting next to me and her laughter fills my ears. She has a joyful look on her face that I haven't seen for a long while. Her expression convinces me that we can get through the demons she's battling, we can get her back to the person she once was. The horses slow down, trotting at a steady pace, before they come to a halt.

As we all climb out of the red sleigh, the children are talking at the tops of their voices and I have to remind them to quieten down so the horses aren't frightened by their noise. The sleigh driver allows us all to give the handsome horses a pat before we move on. And I leave feeling elated that the excursion was a success.

'Are you ready for the next part?' I say, and everyone turns to me with expectant faces. 'We're in France, so what do we absolutely have to do?' I tease.

I clock a few puzzled expressions but Sasha cuts in with the answer I'm looking for. 'Eat lots of cheese!'

'Right the first time.' I rub my hands in anticipation. 'We're going to a fancy French restaurant where the options are cheese, cheese and more cheese!'

Sasha cheers and the others follow suit. Within twenty minutes, we're seated and the waiting staff are incredibly attentive. I order a coffee to warm myself up from the cold temperatures outside. Wrapping my hands around the mug, I don't even need to check the menu because I've memorised the selections I want to have. I'm going to start off strong with a camembert and plenty of bread and chutney to go with it.

'This is the best afternoon, thanks for organising it, Mom.' Leah plants a kiss on my cheek. I glow a little inside, pleased that my efforts have created a memorable time for everyone.

As we begin working our way through a mountain of cheese, my phone rings. I don't answer it because I'm on holiday and family time is the most important thing to me. Besides, all the people I care about are here with me and, if it's anything urgent, the caller will leave a message.

Savouring the creamy deliciousness of the camembert, I scoop another spoonful onto a round cracker and top it off with caramelised red onion chutney. The taste combinations are heavenly.

But I'm distracted now as my phone is ringing again. Perhaps this is an emergency call.

I dig the phone out of the deep pocket of my ski trousers and check the screen. The display on the caller ID shows the name of the last person in the world I want to speak to. So I switch the phone setting to vibrate and let the call ring out before turning off my mobile completely.

I'm not going to let anything or anyone interrupt our family holiday.

Chapter Sixteen

Erin

Leah flicks her short, blonde bob and looks nervously around her. Sasha and our mother have herded the children back to the chalet for their bedtimes, leaving Leah and me to spend some more time in the ski village.

'Are you looking for someone?' I tease, assuming that Leah is scanning the traditional alpine bar to see if her new beau is in the vicinity.

Leah startles. 'What? No, why would I be?'

'Dear sister,' my tone is sincere. 'It's not hard to see that you've got a thing for Xavier Knight – so don't even begin to try to deny it.' I laugh and then do a sweep of the other revellers in the room. Xavier is tall and striking, so if he was nearby I'm sure that one of us would've spotted him by now.

My eyes land on the big stag's head, hanging above the roaring fireplace. I recoil in my rattan seat and quickly look away. I've always hated that piece of decor. It's so outdated, I wish they'd remove it. It jars, especially now there are vegan options on the bar menu. I might have a word with the management about it. I happen to know the owner of the ski resort very well so he might give me the time of day, especially given the rave reviews I've been getting on the refurbishment of Burcott House in the last year.

We've been building up a strong reputation as a boutique hotel but I'm apprehensive about whether Aaron's death is going to impact the business. I cancelled all the bookings in January and February because, given the circumstances, it wasn't appropriate for the hotel to remain open. But I fully intend to relaunch in the next few months once things have blown over. I just hope people aren't uncomfortable staying in a building where a murder has taken place.

'Xavier…' Leah exhales. 'Yes, he's cute.'

'Oh, come on. You think he's more than cute.'

'OK, OK!' Leah holds her hands up. 'I'm into him.'

Picking up my glass of white wine with a flourish, I give her an *I told you so* look.

'He said he would be in this bar tonight.'

'Ah, so that's why you were keen to come in here.'

Leah nods, but she doesn't elaborate any further. She looks a little downcast. Perhaps it's the pressure of the initial dating phase that's got her out of sorts.

'There's something else though…' Leah starts to say and then stops, tracing a finger over the scar on the side of her face without being aware that she's doing it. I've seen her unconsciously touching her scar like this a few times in the past month – it's something she does when she's uncertain or nervous.

I wait to let her continue. There's evidently something on her mind and I don't want to force her to speak until she's ready, in case she clams up.

'I've been having some issues… with a stalker.'

The whole story comes tumbling out of Leah's mouth. She tells me how she made a poor romantic choice and now she's being blackmailed as a result. None of what she's saying surprises me, it was an honest error in judgement on her behalf and now she's paying the price. But I am startled when she tells me the final element of her predicament.

'They're here. At the ski resort. They've followed me.'

'Here?' I look around instantly, as though expecting for the pair of scammers to jump out on us. 'Are you sure?'

'They were at the spa restaurant at lunchtime, both of them.' Leah's mouth is set in a grim line. 'I think Lindsay may even have stolen my cosmetics bag...'

'You've certainly got yourself into a complicated situation.' So she's not just distressed over her missing cosmetics bag because of the hundreds of pounds worth of carefully selected beauty products that have been lost, Leah's concerned there's a sinister meaning behind the missing items.

'What do I do, Erin? I can't keep paying them because soon I won't have anything left. And I don't trust them anyway. Even if I do give them more, they'll soon be harassing me again.'

'And you've not gone to the police? Informed your lawyer?'

Leah shakes her head. 'I thought they would just go away...'

'Well, I'm glad you've told me. I can help.'

'You can?' Leah's big blue eyes are full of hope.

I nod and take another sip of my drink. I'm connected to enough people that I can chase these two off my little sister. I'm confident of that.

'Erin,' Leah hisses between her teeth. 'They're over there.'

Swivelling my head towards the bar, I immediately work out who she means. Shane is hot, I'll give him that. And Lindsay herself is well put together. I'm sure Leah's money has had something to do with that.

Without wasting a second, I stand up and march towards them. Leah is trying to tug me backwards but I get the feeling the direct approach is the only way to tackle this.

'Lindsay, Shane.' I nod to them both, as though we're already acquainted. 'I'm told we have a problem.'

Shane looks like a rabbit caught in the headlights – so this scheme is unlikely to be of his making – but Lindsay faces me with the air of someone who is determined to get what they want.

I lay it out simply for them. I'm going to book them flights home for first thing tomorrow and they need to be on the plane, otherwise I'm going to cause them trouble.

Lindsay is weighing me up, working out how far she can push my buttons. She smirks at me.

'Sorry not possible, I have a ski lesson booked in the morning. And Leah knows what we want.'

Folding my arms across my chest, I raise my eyebrows. 'You've had everything you're going to get from Leah. End of.'

Lindsay starts bleating about exposing my sister as a marriage wrecker online, telling the world about her affair with Shane. I can see why Leah's found it difficult to shake Lindsay off, but I'm having none of it.

I bend down so my mouth is level with Lindsay's ear and I whisper to her, 'My father is in prison for multiple murders. He knows the kind of people you'd never want to meet. He could make you disappear like this –' I click my fingers sharply.

It has the desired effect and she goes pale.

'Is that clear?' I say, as I stand up.

'Crystal,' Lindsay bites back at me. She springs to her feet and grabs Shane's arm, growling at him to follow her. Poor Shane looks utterly perplexed, confusion in his eyes as he's dragged out of the bar by his dragon of a wife.

I make a show of dusting my hands as I return to Leah. 'Job done.'

'Seriously?' Leah gapes at me in astonishment. 'What did you say to her?'

'That's for me to know,' I tap my nose. 'They won't be bothering you again.'

Leah throws her arms around me. 'Thank you, thank you, thank you!' she gushes. 'The whole thing with them has been stressing me out.'

'Make sure you avoid losers like Shane in the future,' I caution her. 'And if you need help again, come to me.'

'I will.' Leah grins. 'It's good having you back Erin.'

Her words warm me. While I still have my issues with my mother and Sasha, I've always felt terrible about Leah's accident. She's grown up a lot in the last ten years; no longer the gawky teenager who was forever stealing my clothes and following me around. I'm proud of the successful person she's become and the potential she has to keep soaring. Leah could become a proper ally for me. I just need to take her under my wing and make sure there are enough reasons for her to stick by my side. Getting rid of Shane and Lindsay is going to keep me in Leah's good books for a while. And I'm sure I can be her confidante and a helping hand in her blossoming relationship with Xavier.

Just as I'm thinking this, Xavier himself materialises at the bar looking dashing in a cable-knit jumper, ski jacket and tight-fitting trousers.

It strikes me that Xavier and Shane have similar looks – both golden boys with athletic bodies. Leah definitely has a type. I just hope Xavier is going to cause her less trouble. Xavier kisses me on the cheek first and then Leah. She flushes red in such a flustered way, which makes her attraction to Xavier more than apparent.

'Would you like a drink?' Xavier asks me.

'No, but thanks for the offer,' I say appreciatively.

Xavier places an order for himself and for Leah. And then my sister excuses herself – I'm guessing she's going to check if the new foundation she hastily purchased in the ski village is doing its job.

Xavier and I make small talk, exchanging news about friends and the ski resort in the easy way of people who've known each other for years. When Leah doesn't return immediately, I cheekily tell Xavier that I think he and my sister are going to make a good pairing.

A slow smile spreads across his face, somewhat predictably. But then he swiftly checks Leah isn't making her way back to us and very smoothly, in a low voice, says something that makes my blood run cold.

'What did you just say?' Disbelief ringing in my ears. Only minutes ago I was warning someone off Leah and now I'm the one who's being threatened.

'You heard me, Erin Bailey-Scott.'

Xavier sucks in a breath and then repeats, 'I know you helped to murder Aaron.'

For once, I'm speechless.

'This has nothing to do with Leah. I like her a lot but you'll appreciate that I need to look after my own interests as well. I'm sure we can come to some sort of financial arrangement.'

I'm reeling. I thought Xavier was one of the very few decent guys. What he's just said convinces me all the more that no man is ever to be trusted.

'Are you behind the messages in the snow?' I snarl at him.

The same sickening smile spreads across his face again. It was him.

Before I can say any more, Leah sashays back to join us and the chance for me to retaliate further has passed. The room suddenly feels very claustrophobic and I have no desire to stay in the same space as Xavier.

'Leah, I'm going to head back...' I announce. 'I'm not feeling great.' In a way it's true, Xavier has just knocked my whole world off-kilter. He knows too much. And he intends to use this to his advantage. I have to try and prise Leah away from him.

'Oh.' Leah looks crestfallen but I know she'll offer to do the right thing. 'Shall I walk you back?'

'Yes, please,' I respond, shrugging on my coat.

I'm also playing off the knowledge that my little sister is currently feeling hugely grateful to me for warning off her stalkers and is more likely to accompany me back to the chalet for this reason.

Leah shrugs and gives her apologies to Xavier, who's regarding me with suspicion in his eyes.

'I'll come with you ladies,' Xavier offers chivalrously.

'There's no need for that,' I say firmly.

'It's my pleasure.'

And so I find myself being escorted back to Snowfall Chalet by both Leah and Xavier.

There's no opportunity to warn my sister off Xavier as the three of us walk in step with each other and far too soon the chalet comes into view.

'Here we are,' Xavier announces as we stand outside my holiday home.

'Are you ok?' Leah asks, her blue eyes full of concern.

'No... I think I've got a migraine coming on.' I put my hand to my forehead to reinforce my words.

'Bed is the best thing for you then,' Xavier says confidently, as though he's some kind of expert.

I watch as he clasps Leah's hand in his. He says to her, 'It's still early, so I was thinking we could go back to my chalet. A few of my friends are there and, knowing them, the apres-ski will be in full swing by now.'

Leah flushes and nods in response. She turns to me, 'Is there anything I can get you before I go?'

'Well –'

'I'm sure your sister just needs some peace and quiet,' Xavier interrupts, not allowing me another opportunity to try and get Leah on her own.

I narrow my eyes at him. There's nothing I can say to stop Leah heading back out into the night with the man she's fast becoming besotted with and he knows it. At least not without admitting to her that Xavier knows the truth about Aaron's death.

I'm certain no harm will come to her though. Xavier's problem isn't with Leah and at no point has he said he wants to expose my crime. From what I can tell, he just wants money. A rumour has been flying round that he squandered his grandfather's inheritance a bit too fast, so the need for some more funds would tally with this. I'm still trying to analyse the words he so bluntly delivered earlier on as he smirks at me and waves goodbye.

Standing on the snow-covered doorstep, I keep my eyes on Xavier and Leah as they merge back into the throng of people making their way to and from the ski village. They soon melt into the crowd. Easing my gloves off, I place them into the right-hand pocket of my jacket but, as I do so, I feel the shape of something else tucked in there.

I yank out a screwed-up piece of paper. I unfold it hastily and instantly know that, like the messages in the snow, these words are from Xavier. Scrawled on the paper is the sentence:

I KNOW YOUR SECRET.

Chapter Seventeen
Sasha

As soon as I open the door to the main bar, the noise level hits me and I almost retreat and turn back to the chalet. Instead, I take a deep breath and step inside. I'd prefer to be sitting in front of the sofa, scrolling on my phone, but my mum insisted I join Erin and Leah for a child-free evening once the little ones had gone to sleep. As I walked here, the snowflakes were falling heavily so I had my hood up around my face. I was lost in a daydream, a pretence that everything was normal and that Jesse was here with me at the ski resort. I shouldn't let my mind roam down the path of 'what if?' because it's not going to do me any good – and it certainly won't change the reality I've found myself in. I shrug off my coat now and dislodge the snow that's settled on my clothing.

Wandering around the busy bar, I search for my two sisters. They were here about an hour and a half ago and I just assumed they'd be in the same spot. I didn't think to call them to say I was coming to join them. But I can't see either of them and, after a fruitless five minutes, I debate whether to just leave. They may well have moved on somewhere else or they might even have walked back to the chalet. I could easily have missed them on the way here as the figures walking past me were equally bundled up in warm layers. I send a quick message to check where they are.

'Excuse me,' a woman with long, wavy hair says as I hover by her table. 'Are you waiting for someone?'

'I'm just looking for my sisters. I was hoping to meet them here.'

She ushers me into a seat. 'I'm waiting as well. My date hasn't shown up yet so I'd love some company while I'm sitting here.'

'Oh no, how late is your date?' I ask. The woman looks slightly flustered and I feel sorry for her if she's about to be stood up.

I don't think I could enter the world of modern dating, even if I wanted to. Jesse and I met through mutual friends but that doesn't happen often these days. So many of my younger colleagues have met their partners by swiping left – or is it right? – on dating apps. Blind dates and exchanging messages with someone you've never met before are the norm. I never thought I'd be in a position where the possibility of dating opened up to me once more. I was sure that I was married for life. Right now, meeting someone else is not something I can even contemplate. And, judging by the tortured expression on my companion's face, I'm not sure it will be something that I ever want to consider again.

The woman checks her smartwatch. 'He's about fifteen minutes past the time we agreed.'

'May have just got held up then, I'll join you for a bit but will disappear as soon as the person you're waiting for arrives.'

'Thank you.' She has a slight Australian accent but it's only now that I'm sitting opposite her that I detect it.

She pours me a glass of water from the tall jug on the table and then checks her watch again. 'I can't believe he's not turned up.'

'I'm sure he'll be here soon enough,' I try to reassure her. I'm not in the habit of chatting with strangers, but at least this will allow me a five-minute stop before I go back out into the elements. I check my phone but there's no response from either Erin or Leah in our 'Sisters' messaging group.

'I was going to leave earlier on... I had a nasty encounter with someone in this bar. But I decided not to let it ruin my trip.' The woman swirls ice around her glass. 'My name's Lindsay by the way.'

'I'm Sasha,' I respond. 'Nice to meet you.'

'Are you a regular at this resort?'

I shake my head. 'It's my first time here.'

'Me too,' Lindsay tells me. 'I feel a bit like a fish out of water to be honest. I'm not much of a skier.'

Lindsay seems nice, chatty and friendly. And it sounds like she's having a tough day. So I don't mind passing the time with her.

'I'm quite rusty,' I confide in her. 'I need to get some confidence back.' As the words escape my lips, it strikes me that this is true for a lot of aspects of my life, not just skiing. I used to be so sure of myself, what happened?

The door crashes open and Lindsay automatically swings her head in the direction of the sound. An older woman comes through the door and Lindsay sighs.

'It's snowing pretty hard out there, perhaps it's delayed him.' Memories of my own failed dates in the past come flooding back to me.

'My date is my husband,' Lindsay shares with me. 'We're at a make-or-break stage, so I really thought he'd make an effort.'

She looks as though she's about to cry, so I lay a hand over hers. 'I'm sure he'll be here soon enough,' I soothe.

'I'm not so convinced...' Lindsay has a faraway look in her eyes. 'You see, he cheated on me.'

A tear trickles down her cheek and she covers her face with her hands to hide it. I don't know what to say but I immediately feel an affinity with this woman after the way Jesse betrayed me. He may not have cheated in the physical sense – or at least not as far as I know – but he fell in love with someone else and that still hurts.

'I'm so sorry...' I take a swig of water and then say, 'I understand what you're going through.'

Lindsay wipes the tears from her eyes and stares at me curiously, 'Have you been cheated on as well?'

I squirm in my seat; it's the first time I've said any of this out loud to anyone. 'Sort of... in the emotional sense.'

Lindsay gives herself a little shake. 'I think we both need a drink!'

I start to protest but she's already making her way to the bar. I tell myself I'll just have one, to keep Lindsay company, because it feels like she needs it.

We clink glasses and I take a small sip of the cocktail she's handed to me. Lindsay glances round the room again. 'Well, I think this is officially the end of my marriage.'

My sympathy goes out to this poor woman. I can't imagine being stood up by my husband on a date that's been arranged in an attempt to save the marriage. It really sucks that Lindsay's in this position. It also gives me some perspective – I'm not the only one going through a break-up.

'Do you want to talk about it?' I ask her.

She purses her lips. 'There's not much to say. We've been married for six years. It's the classic seven-year itch on the horizon. I found out he'd been cheating on me with some platinum blonde...'

'That's terrible.'

'How about you?' Lindsay looks at me with curiosity in her eyes.

'Um, it's a bit complicated. But we're not together anymore.' I'm not about to divulge to a complete stranger that my husband is now in prison for murder. That may scare her off. This is something I'm going to have to deal with for the rest of my life. My connection to Jesse is going to become a source of shame, something to keep secret. I realise the sooner we divorce, the better. Then I can start to put him behind me.

'Half an hour,' Lindsay declares. 'He's not coming, is he?'

I don't want to be the one to confirm her fears, but I think she's correct. 'There may be a valid reason but, if not, what are you going to do?'

'What I should've done months ago. Leave our marriage.' She drains her drink. 'I should never have given him a second chance. He gave the usual excuses – she chased him, it meant nothing – but I can't forgive him.'

'You're better off without him.' I realise this is true for my own circumstances. 'Here, let's raise a toast... To strong women!'

'Strong women!' Lindsay echoes, as we clink glasses.

I go and get some more drinks. I owe Lindsay one, I reason to myself, and I'll stop as soon as I've had this.

Once I'm settled at the table again, I notice that Lindsay has shed a few more tears. 'It doesn't help that she was younger, thinner... all the things you dread. She's even a successful businesswoman. One of those influencers. No wonder his head was turned.'

'Hey, it's on him and not on you.'

We talk more, putting the world to rights, but my heart misses a beat when Lindsay says, 'You're right, I've had a lucky escape. Perhaps I should be thanking Leah Bailey.'

'Leah Bailey?'

'Yep, that's the name of the woman he cheated with.'

There's no way I can hide my flabbergasted reaction. Leah had an affair? With the husband of the woman I'm randomly sitting with?

'Do you know her?' Lindsay asks.

'She's my sister!' I blurt out. As soon as I say this, it dawns on me that I could've pretended to be one of her followers and I didn't have to admit to such a close connection.

'Your sister!' Lindsay visibly flinches.

I find myself telling Lindsay that I haven't seen Leah for a long time, until recently, because she's been living in Australia. I express that I don't condone her behaviour in any way. I'm staggered to hear my little sister has been having a relationship with a married man. She's got everything going for her, so why did she feel the need to steal another woman's husband?

I apologise on behalf of Leah, telling Lindsay I'm going to confront my younger sister about her behaviour.

Lindsay shakes her head. 'It's not your fault, you're not her keeper and, from what you've said, you guys haven't been that close recently. Besides, you've been where I am. You and me, we're in the same boat.'

More drinks end up being ordered. I can't exactly leave Lindsay now, not when she's so low and I've just dropped this bombshell on her. The time ticks on and I forget all about going to find Erin and Leah. Lindsay and I are like lost souls who've serendipitously found each other. She's not mad about my connection to Leah and we end up talking like old friends.

My resolve to not consume as much alcohol today soon goes out the window. Before long, I've lost track of how much I've had. But I've made a new friend and it's good for me to be bonding with someone who's going through marital difficulties and, by the sounds of it, also heading for divorce.

I end up telling Lindsay about my family and all about Jesse and the Christmas party. The whole sorry story comes spilling out. Lindsay is a good audience and dishes out appropriate responses in all the right places as I unburden myself on her. I find myself nodding in agreement to everything she has to say. Her opinions on how everyone behaved are a refreshing new perspective. She asks me questions about Leah and about Erin while topping up my glass.

Somehow, it's liberating to talk to a stranger about what I've been through. I've been holding everything in, going over and over my conversations with Jesse in the last few months, trying to process the way he behaved when the police arrested him. Saying my husband betrayed me out loud makes what happened feel more real; the sequence of events solidifies in my mind and I finally experience a rush of emotions crashing through me, after feeling numb for so long.

Lindsay stopped drinking a little while ago, but I finish off our bottle of wine and order another, slipping on the sticky wooden flooring as I make my way back from the bar again. I only just catch myself from falling because of a conveniently placed bar stool. Lindsay's face swims in front of me and I'm not sure if she's sneering or smiling.

I know I shouldn't, but I pour another glass full to the brim. I'm on a roll now, heading on a downward trajectory that I'm unable to stop.

Chapter Eighteen

Leah

Should I feel impressed or intimidated by the way Erin dealt with Shane and Lindsay? I'm surprised she managed to get them to back off but I also ponder over what she whispered in Lindsay's ear to make her go so quickly. Should I be thankful? Or should I be scared of the power my sister appears to have?

Either way, it feels like a huge weight has been removed from my shoulders knowing that Lindsay and Shane have been told to leave the resort. I feel like I can breathe properly again and, as I turn away from Snowfall Chalet, with my arm linked with Xavier's, I suck in the refreshing mountain air.

'This snow is getting heavy,' I remark. The snowflakes are coming down so thick and fast that the landscape is starting to blur a little.

'My chalet isn't too far,' Xavier tells me.

I allow him to lead the way. When we walk through the door to his cabin, it's clear the apres-ski really is in full swing. There are clusters of people gathered in the open-plan room, which has exactly the same layout as Snowfall Chalet. For some reason, I assumed the accommodation at this exclusive ski resort would be more bespoke but the interior is almost identical to Erin's cabin, aside from the decor.

Music blasts from a boombox and I spot Isla dancing enthusiastically in a bright pink ensemble. Fernando is part of the same crowd, he's leaning back casually, vaping as he watches Isla moving to the beat. I'm now certain that it was Lindsay who sent the photograph of Xavier and me in The Ice Bar to my phone, so I'm not worried about either of them being an issue. But I still think Fernando is a sleazeball.

Xavier hands me a glowing, garish-coloured shot. We clink the little glasses and I drink quickly, the sour taste hitting my tongue. Xavier smiles wolfishly at me, and then he leans in and kisses me. It takes me by surprise; I wasn't expecting him to make his move the minute we walked through the door. He pulls me down onto a sofa that's been pushed up against the window, and I lose myself in the physical contact. We kiss hungrily and Xavier whispers sweet nothings in my ear.

The music and the drinking ramps up a notch. I find myself on the makeshift dance floor, pressed close to Xavier, his strong arms around me. It feels good to be here with him. Again, I can't stop myself from speculating if this is the start of something exciting between us. If Xavier could be more than just a kiss, if he could be my future. I twist and twirl, dancing with Isla and Fernando, and then with Xavier again. Slowly, people begin to peel off and the party starts to wind down. I go to the bathroom and when I come back, Xavier has gone from the main room. I get a drink and sit down, my head spinning slightly. I wait for him but thirty minutes pass and he still doesn't reappear. My eyes grow heavy and I begin to doze in my seat.

Fernando comes to sit on the sofa beside me, jolting me awake. 'You OK?'

I nod unconvincingly.

'Xavier disappeared?' The smell of beer is heavy on his breath.

'Yeah... I may make a move.'

'He's probably just fallen asleep somewhere, that would be so like him.'

I get the feeling that Fernando is trying to make me feel better. Perhaps I misjudged him. I'm guessing that Xavier has got distracted by something – or someone – else. I scan the room and note that Isla is nowhere to be seen either. I'm not prepared to wait around to find out what Xavier's getting up to, so I say my goodbyes to Fernando and stand up.

'Are you walking back? I'll come with you.' He goes to push himself up from the sofa.

'No, it's fine. Thanks for the offer but I'm only a five-minute walk.' There's still something about Fernando that makes me feel uncomfortable. I'd rather walk by myself than with him.

'If you're sure?' Fernando says. 'Just don't go wandering off the path!'

Thanking him again, I locate my big ski coat and put on my outer layers. If I speed walk back then I can be in my bed in under fifteen minutes. Outside it's dark and the coldest temperature I've experienced on the trip so far. I lightly jog, partly to keep myself warm and party to get back sooner. As I arrive at Snowfall Chalet, a message pings on my phone. It's Xavier: *Where are you?*

I'm too tired now to reply. All I know is that he disappeared for almost an hour and I need some rest. I crawl into bed without responding and I bury my head in the pillow, willing sleep to come.

***

When I wake up, I've had several more messages from Xavier and a number of missed calls. I check my watch. I've only been in bed for a couple of short hours but I haven't been able to rest properly. There's something niggling in my mind, something that doesn't feel right.

As I turn the events of the previous evening over in my mind, I feel guilty about running out of the party. Perhaps I jumped to conclusions about Xavier way too quickly? As I toss and turn, it becomes apparent there's no way I'm going to get any kind of proper sleep. My body is too charged with adrenaline and sugar from the food and drink I had yesterday.

I'm still dressed, having collapsed into my bed fully clothed, so I get up and check myself in the mirror. My make up is smudged but there's not much I can do about that as I still haven't found the missing cosmetics bag. I could do with a shower as well but I've made my mind up to head back to Xavier's chalet. It's not too far from here and I want to find out where he went last night. Something feels odd about it and I want to know exactly what happened. He was being so attentive towards me so it was strange for him to then just vanish.

Did he really go off with Isla? Is there something going on between the two of them? Or am I just reading too much into Isla being nowhere to be found as well? I want to get to the bottom of it because, the truth is, I could fall very hard for Xavier if I let myself. But I don't want there to be any silly games between us. I want to know if he's for real. And I have to know now.

Silence.

Outside, all I can hear is silence.

The world around me is hazy. Crisp, fresh snow, several inches deep, crunches under my heavy boots. The icy caps of the mountain peaks tower above me, looking monochrome and chilling in the dim light. I inhale the cold air in short, sharp breaths as my eyes adjust to the gloom. The darkness of the night is only just beginning to lift and the sun is still yet to rise.

It's a long time since I've been up this early. And it's eerie, standing here by myself in the middle of this exclusive ski resort without a soul nearby. I'm used to seeing this scene brimming with people in colourful outfits, laughter and chatter swirling in the air around me. But not even the chalet girls are up.

I retrace the steps that I'd trodden only hours before, making my way slowly down the slippery path. My mouth is dry and my whole body feels sluggish, but I keep going. I need to fill in the missing puzzle pieces of my memories from last night. The apres-ski was in full swing and the drinks kept on flowing. As I slip and slide down the hillside, snapshots of the evening flicker in my mind. Dancing close, that kiss and then...

I need to talk to Xavier.

As the cold makes me wish I'd wrapped up warmer, my phone vibrates in my pocket. I pull it out to see a stream of notifications across social media platforms. There are also five missed calls from Xavier and a multitude of unopened messages from him. I click into my message app and the words that leap out at me make the hairs on the back of my neck stand on end. My mind whirrs as I try to take in the information Xavier has shared with me.

Looking up from my electronic device, I reach the large chalet where I last saw Xavier. I'm not sure I can go in there anymore. I'm not sure I can face him after the secret he's shared with me. Because the sentence I've just read has shifted my world on its axis.

Despite the news changing everything, in my bones I know it's the truth. My teeth are chattering as I stand frozen, wondering whether to take a few strides forwards to Xavier's chalet or whether to turn on my heel and delay the inevitable conversation that I need to have.

I notice there's a gap around the door of the chalet, it's not fully shut. Not so long ago this place was teeming with people so maybe someone carelessly forgot to close it. A shiver runs through me. It must be freezing inside. I hope there's a simple explanation but a feeling of dread creeps over me. I don't think the answer is going to be that simple. Bracing myself, I push open the heavy wooden door. Stepping inside, I survey the scene. The wreckage of the night before is plain to see. Beer cans, pizza boxes and wine bottles clutter every surface. A chair is upturned and clothes are strewn everywhere. But there's no one here. There's nothing but silence. Everyone is long gone.

I briefly wonder where Isla and Fernando are. I'm sure they were staying at this chalet with Xavier. They could be crashed out in bed or maybe they've gone on to another party. I'm turning to go, feeling foolish for coming back here, when I see something out of the corner of my eye, snagging my attention. I turn fully towards the heap of material in the centre of the room.

And that's when I realise... it's not just a jumble of clothing, there's a person lying there. It's Xavier.

'Xavier?'

There's no response so I drop to my knees and brush the hair off his face with my gloved hand.

I gasp, my jaw dropping in shock.

He is too cold, too pale, too lifeless.

The door is still open, and a cold blast of wind sweeps into the room, causing snowflakes to flutter into the chalet. I feel numb. This can't be real.

I look back down and that's when I see it.

The knife. And the blood.

My worst fears are confirmed and I step back with a cry. Panic grips me. I can't be found here.

I rush outside, my breath catching in my chest as I force myself back up the hillside. One thought circling in my mind:

What really happened last night?

Chapter Nineteen

Nadia

Yesterday was perfect. An indulgent spa morning, followed by an enchanting sleigh ride, rounded off with French wine and cheese. I'm holding onto the knowledge that I did everything I could to make sure my family had a special day. Everything I do is for them. Seeing my girls looking more relaxed and my grandchildren smiling has been a relief. Maybe this holiday can be the balm this family needs to help us recharge and give us strength for the coming months. But the efforts of making sure my family are well-looked after are starting to take their toll on me. I barely slept a wink last night.

I pull another load of washing out of the tumble dryer and then busy myself with making sure the children's rucksacks are filled with everything they could possibly need for a day on the slopes: spare gloves, drinks, tissues, plenty of healthy snacks and a secret stash of biscuits from their nana. Today we're heading back out for ski lessons. I know Freya is nervous, so I write her a quick note of encouragement on a fluorescent orange Post-it note and attach it to her sandwiches.

I can't wait to get out onto the snow again. I loved the feeling of working my muscles, the wind in my hair, and I'm looking forward to doing it all over again. Grabbing the suncream, I remember to slather a generous amount on my face. I don't want to return home with visor marks, thank you very much.

I'm determined that we're going to have an equally brilliant day today and make even more special memories. Yes, I'm probably fixating on this but it's important to me. The fallout from Aaron's death has been enormous and we've all handled our emotions in very different ways. And I know that things are likely to get harder because Jesse's crown court date is looming. It's been delayed due to the Christmas holidays and a general backlog, but we should know at the end of February what his sentence is. As he's pleading guilty, he should get a reduction in the amount of time he spends in prison, and because he's intending to say it wasn't pre-planned and his judgement was impaired by alcohol those factors should also be taken into consideration. But, the fact is, he killed a man. He's going to go to prison for a very long time and there's no telling how Sasha and Freya will react once the reality is confirmed. Leah was also close to Jesse – they were like brother and sister – and she's going to be rocked once the court ruling is decided as well.

I exhale slowly and try to distract myself from my racing thoughts. I set to work on filling my own rucksack for the day. I make sure to pack my spare sunscreen and double check the first aid kit is still wedged in the front compartment of my bag, along with a second purse containing emergency money. I like to plan for every eventuality. Often, this pays off, but sometimes I get it wrong.

My mind turns to Erin. To the outside world she is a grieving widow and Jesse is her husband's killer. So therefore Jesse's sentence should have a very different meaning for her. It should mean the day justice is served for Aaron.

Except, I know that's not the truth.

I saw Erin as she encouraged Jesse to fight back against Aaron. I'm not sure she intended for Jesse to take things as far as he did. But I also saw her calmly walk past her husband's dead body without a shred of emotion. She is just as guilty as Jesse is but she's walked away without consequence.

This is partly because of me. I sit down heavily in a chair. I know I'm not blameless in all of this. I stayed quiet on that awful night. I didn't say a word because I didn't want Erin to go to prison, or for her children to suffer any more than they already are in the wake of their father's death. I also couldn't even begin to imagine how messed up it would be if the twins found out their mother engineered their father's murder.

I run my hands through my short blonde hair. This is all because Erin and Jesse decided to risk everything because they wanted to be together. I managed to put a stop to the affair between them ten years ago. I'd thought Erin and Jesse's feelings for each other were in the past. I had no idea they'd reignited things between them again. If I'd had any inkling, I would've done something about it.

As things worked out, they didn't get away with their plan to secretly kill Aaron. I saw what they did and when the police questioned me, I gave them Jesse's name. He confessed to everything, in order to protect Erin. I was surprised about this; perhaps they really do have deep feelings for each other. But the truth must stay buried. Not just for Erin's sake but also for Sasha's sake and for the sake of my innocent grandchildren. Sasha still knows nothing about her husband and sister's betrayal; she believes Jesse was just infatuated with Erin.

As the children come barrelling into the room with wide smiles, eager for their breakfasts, I know it's up to me to make sure they're shielded from the terrible truth. And it's up to me to sort out Erin and make sure she never, ever makes choices like that again. Because I can't keep covering up things for her. If there's a next time, I might not be able to save her.

'Can I have Nana's porridge?' Jasper asks, a mischievous glint in his eye. 'You make it the best.'

I laugh. 'Of course you can, you're a growing lad.'

I wash my hands vigorously several times before pouring some milk into the pan. Getting the children ready for the day is a task that's fallen to me. But I don't mind, it's a pleasure to get the three of them set up and I'm enjoying spending time with them.

'Good morning, love,' I say to Erin. Sometimes it's hard to keep my interactions with her normal, when so often I get the urge to shake her for being so reckless. But I'm biding my time and I'm going to deal with Erin in my own way so that nothing like Aaron's death and Jesse's imprisonment ever happens again.

Erin has her copper hair twisted up in a messy bun. Her green eyes look even brighter thanks to the eye make-up she has on, and she looks gorgeous in an emerald-green all-in-one ski suit.

'What a beautiful colour outfit,' I remark.

'I do like the shade of this one,' Erin agrees. She gives the twins a peck on the cheek and ruffles Freya's flame-red hair.

My mind strays to my first love – Sasha and Erin's father, Craig Turner. Not for the first time, I think that Craig has made his mark on this family without even being here. Craig has the same copper colouring as Erin, and both the twins and Freya have inherited this gene from him as well.

The missed call I had yesterday, it was from him. It was from Craig.

Every so often, I get a letter or a phone call from where he resides at His Majesty's pleasure. I make visits to him, as infrequently as I can get away with. We had a rule that if I kept him updated on Sasha and Erin then he wouldn't interfere with their lives. He's kept his word as far as I know but the amount of contact I've had from him has increased this year. He knows about Aaron's death and Jesse's arrest. And he's making it his business to dig deeper into what really happened. But Craig is the least of my problems. I'm not going to get back to him while I'm away from home, however much it irritates him. It'll keep. After all, he's behind bars.

Jasper has finished his porridge and is now climbing into his ski suit. Once done, he begins chasing Freya around the room. They rush about, their voices becoming more and more high-pitched as they crash into pieces of furniture and knock things over.

'Enough!' Erin says firmly. She raises her voice but doesn't shout. The children stop immediately and the situation is instantly calms down. Freya is still giggling into her hand as Jasper is pulling funny faces but they're a lot calmer than they were. I wish I had that kind of commanding influence when I was a mother to young children – perhaps that's where things started going awry with my brood.

Sasha has now joined us and, for a fleeting moment, I think it's odd that Leah isn't up already. She's usually an early riser.

'Freya, can you go and give Auntie Leah a wake-up call please.'

Freya bounds off, with Jasper hot on her heels, and I hear them squealing in the corridor before they burst into Leah's bedroom. I'm sure that will do the trick.

I'm clearing away the plates when I hear a knock at the door.

'I'll get it,' I say to Erin. I'm expecting it to be Marnie, the nice lady from across the way. She's about my age, so it would be good to chat to her a bit more and make a friend out here.

Pausing in the hallway, I check myself in the mirror. I look presentable enough, despite the lack of sleep.

Opening the blue front door, I fix a welcoming smile on my face. But my expression rapidly turns to horror.

Because it's not Marnie standing on the snowy doorstep. I drop the cup I'm still holding and it shatters on the floor.

This must be a nightmare. It can't be real.

'Aren't you going to invite me in then?'

The rough accent, the devious smile, the copper-coloured hair. I'm not hallucinating.

Craig Turner is standing right in front of me.

Chapter Twenty

Erin

'Am I pleased to see you.'

He's here. He's *finally* here. Craig Turner, my father, is out of prison. I didn't think I'd feel quite so emotional about his arrival, but I do. He opens his arms and we embrace.

'Welcome to Snowfall Chalet,' I say.

Stepping out of his arms, I catch sight of my mother standing in the doorway. She looks horrified, just as I expected she would. Craig's release from prison was not on her radar at all. But she's not the only one who can keep a secret.

'Who's that, Mummy?' Freya asks, a cloud of suspicion on her little face as she looks to Sasha for reassurance.

Sasha's dark hair is frizzy and she's still in her worn blue pyjamas with the hole in the knee. Her lip curls in disdain as she takes in the man standing in the middle of the room.

'It's your grandfather,' I supply.

There's a second of silence as my words sink in.

And then, everyone starts reacting at once.

'He is *not* her grandfather—' Sasha cries.

'Is he our grandfather too?' Ophelia pipes up.

'What's going on?' Leah stumbles into the room, her face a picture of confusion.

Craig laughs, a loud and deep rumble. 'I've only been here five minutes and I'm already causing trouble.'

'Freya, Jasper, Ophelia,' my mother says, 'into your room now, put the TV on. You've got half an hour before we go out.'

Distracted by the prospect of unexpected screen time, the younger generation of the family obediently do as they're told.

Hands on hips, eyes blazing with fury, Nadia confronts Craig. 'What are you doing out of prison?'

Craig chuckles and comes to stand next to me, draping an arm around my shoulder. 'I've got Erin to thank, she's a clever one, isn't she?'

My mother, Sasha and Leah are all wearing the same expressions on their faces: disbelief mixed with fear.

'She helped push my release forward.'

'You said...' Nadia jabs her finger into Craig's chest. 'You said you'd leave the girls alone.'

'I did what you wanted Nadia, for the best part of three decades. But you didn't keep your end of the bargain, did you?'

Nadia folds her arms across her chest. 'What exactly do you mean by that?'

'Erin here hasn't been involved in many family gatherings for the last ten years, has she?'

Nadia blanches.

'So when she reached out to me for help, I wasn't going to turn her away.'

The air around my parents crackles with pent-up feelings and un-said words. It's strange to see them here in the same room. My mother was pregnant with me when Craig was sentenced for murder and I grew up believing that Simon, Leah's dad, was my father too. I discovered this was a lie in my twenties when I overheard my mother talking to Sasha about Craig. I wasn't meant to hear and my mother never realised that I'd found out the truth. She only came clean at my ill-fated Christmas party last year but by that time I'd already formed a strong relationship with my biological father. This is my opportunity to reveal how much of a daddy's girl I've become. It'll be interesting to see how my mother reacts when she realises that she's the one who's been kept in the dark this time.

Nadia backs down first, her shoulders sagging, and she inches away from Craig and goes to stand at the floor-to-ceiling window. Sasha is beside her in a flash, the two of them huddling together against the backdrop of the breathtaking mountains.

Leah throws her hands in the air. 'This has nothing to do with me, so I'll leave you to it.' She heads in the direction of the bedrooms.

Craig's arrival was always going to have an impact, but I'm so happy he made it – and that our plan worked.

'We did it!' I mouth to Craig and he rewards me with a wink.

'Any chance of some food? Drink?' Craig asks.

I snap into action and pour him a coffee before organising some cheese on toast. He grabs a chair at the breakfast bar and makes himself at home. It feels good to finally have someone in the family who's truly on my side.

This has been a long time coming. It's been five years since I first got in contact with my biological father. I found out he was in prison for double murder a little while before that. But, raising two young babies, I didn't initially have the time or the mental energy to be in contact with him. I wasn't even sure I wanted to get to know him. When the twins went to school, I had a bit more headspace to consider things and I decided to reach out and get to know him before passing judgement.

Seeing my father for the first time was like finding a kindred spirit. We look so alike – same straight nose, same smile, same colour hair. I've always felt like the odd one out in my family, my personality just didn't fit with that of my mother or the sisters I grew up with. We were always clashing. And, whenever there was an argument, no one ever understood my point of view. It was like I was from a different planet.

I place the steaming mug of coffee and the toast down in front of him and he rubs his hands together to show his approval. I smile at him sitting just metres from me, in a normal setting without any prison wardens trying to eavesdrop on our conversation. Craig understands me, he gets my sense of humour and my ambition. After we'd got to know each other a bit better, I shared the truth about my marriage. Aaron was controlling and manipulative; the longer I was with him, the less my life felt like my own. I twirl my gold wedding band around my finger. It was never meant to end up like this. When I married Aaron I thought we'd be the perfect couple but that dream faded pretty fast. When I shared what my life was really like with Aaron, my father made me see it was either Aaron or me. I had to do whatever it took to get out of the marriage unscathed.

Jesse was collateral damage, not intentionally, but apart from that glitch the plot to free me from my marriage worked. Craig and I also set a plan in motion two years ago to free him from prison. He'd spent over thirty years in a cell but his sentence hadn't been reduced, despite recent good behaviour. So I had to find another way out for him. Craig knew a lot about the staff as well as the inmates at the prison. We selected our target wisely and, with some assistance from my own contacts, we were able to get Craig's sentence significantly lowered thanks to him cooperating with another enquiry, involving a prison warden. Craig got his first taste of freedom two weeks ago and I was granted special permission for him to be allowed to stay with me at this chalet in France, as part of his rehabilitation pathway. It helped that some money exchanged hands in order to persuade the officials to allow Craig out of the country so soon.

I'm aware Nadia and Sasha are whispering together at the other end of the room. I don't expect springing Craig on everyone is going to go smoothly, but I've got to try to get my mother to at least entertain the idea of him being back in the family fold. It's Craig's greatest wish.

I blink and then Nadia is striding towards us. 'I don't know what you expected to achieve by coming here,' she says to Craig in a shrill voice. 'But whatever it is you want, ask for it now and then go.'

Craig's knife clatters to his plate and he scowls at her. 'What a welcome that is!'

'You lost the right to anything from me years ago.'

'Come on Nadia, all I want is my family back.'

'You should've thought about that before you landed yourself in jail.' Her expression is hard and unsympathetic.

'I've paid the consequences; believe me I have.' Some of the bravado falls away from Craig's face now. 'I just want another chance... is that too much to ask?'

Nadia hesitates and, for a moment, I think she might waver. But then Sasha cuts in.

'Nice try, but no.' Sasha's face is a picture of hatred.

This must be raw for her. She's going through a very similar experience to the one our mother went through thirty years ago. Sasha has been left a single mother while her husband serves time for murder. It's like history is repeating itself.

'Sasha, my girl. You're—' Craig stands up and extends a tattooed arm towards his eldest daughter, but she smacks his hand away.

We all look at her aghast. Sasha is not a violent person so I can't believe she just did that. A small part of me is a little bit afraid about what Craig's response might be. But he simply shrugs and sits back down.

'I've got a lot of making up to do. I get why you're angry with me.'

'I have nothing more to say to you,' Sasha states this in no uncertain terms to Craig. She then turns her attention to Nadia. 'Mum, I'm taking Freya out for the day. Are you coming with us?'

'Yes, you girls get your boots and coats on and I'll come with you.' Nadia gives Sasha a small smile and then turns her attention back on Craig.

'You can't come here and stir things up when—'

I interject. 'Listen, I invited him here. I just want a chance to get to know my father.'

'Erin, I've tried to protect you from him your whole life. Don't get sucked in now, not when you have your own little ones to look after.'

Her words chink my armour. Of course I don't want to do anything to jeopardise my children's happiness. But I believe having my father around will make me happy. And I'm going to help him set himself up for a good life.

'He's staying,' I answer firmly.

Nadia's eyes glisten. 'Sasha and I will go then.'

I didn't think my mother would be this quick to shut the conversation down.

'What about Jasper and Ophelia?'

She hesitates. 'They can come back to England with me.'

I scoff. 'No, they'll be upset. They were looking forward to this holiday. And they're not going anywhere without me.'

'Erin you can't expect me to stay under the same roof as him. Not after what he did.'

'He's changed!' I throw back at her.

She shakes her head and places the palm of her hand on my cheek. 'I wish it wasn't the case... but you'll learn.'

'Nadia, look, let's talk. There's a lot to say—'

Nadia stops Craig's sentence with a shake of her head and then she exits the room.

That introduction didn't exactly go to plan. The little girl inside me just wants to see my parents together. But I knew it was going to be tough to try and get Nadia onside.

'I'm sorry...' I say to Craig.

'It was worth a try.' Craig stares up at the ceiling for a beat and then says, 'So where are those grandkiddies?'

There's movement in the hallway but I don't attempt to stop any of my family leaving. I stand at the front window and observe Nadia, Sasha and Freya spilling outside. Leah is with them too. They pause to exchange a few words, no doubt to work out where they're going next. And then Marnie from the chalet across from ours appears at her front door. I see her engage my family in conversation and it's not long before she ushers all of them inside her warm house. She turns and gives me a little wave before shutting her pink front door.

I smile.

Marnie has been briefed. She's been a useful friend to me. I sent her a message when the others were getting ready to leave.

She knows what to do next.

Chapter Twenty-One

Sasha

'Who is that man?' Freya asks me innocently, as we tumble outside Snowfall chalet.

How do I explain any of this to a girl of just ten years old? My answers are either: 'He's the father I didn't know about until ten years ago,' or, 'He's the grandfather who's spent your whole life in prison.' I'm not sure which Freya would be more confused by. I shiver as we stand in the cold.

'Um... he's someone Nana used to know.' This is technically not untrue. I give the shortest answer possible as I want to move us all away from Erin's chalet. But Freya persists.

'But Auntie Erin said he was my grandfather... Do I really have a grandfather?'

This is another reason to add to my high pile of reasons to dislike Erin. She shouldn't have blurted that out in front of Freya. Jesse doesn't see much of his own parents so Nadia is the only grandparent Freya has a meaningful relationship with. It's confusing for her to suddenly have a grandfather pop up out of the blue.

'Not quite.' I drop a kiss on her head. 'Let's talk about it later.'

I shiver and can feel my nose already turning red in the cold. Leah and mum are talking earnestly about where to go next. I can see my mum is agitated, constantly flicking her gaze back to Snowfall chalet. I'm about to step in with a suggestion when the neighbour who lives opposite Erin comes out of her pink door.

'Hello!' She waves, a bright smile on her face.

'So pleased to see you all again,' she chirps. I remember her name is Marnie. Erin has mentioned her a few times and she's spoken to us as we've made our way in and out of the chalet over the last few days. She behaves like a typical nosey neighbour. I imagine she's probably just lonely, as she always hovering whenever anyone is going by.

'It's freezing out here, would you like to come in for a quick cup of tea?' She directs her question at my mum. 'I've got biscuits as well – and I shouldn't eat them all myself!'

My mum chuckles. 'That's so kind. Actually, yes that would be lovely.'

Marnie's smile gets even broader, if that's possible. She strikes me as being a little too over-friendly and I question if she's in the habit of inviting neighbours in for tea. I guess it's sweet. I don't really want to follow my mum inside but I allow myself to be drawn into Marnie's chalet. It'll give me a chance to process Craig's surprise arrival and to think about what to do next.

'Sugar? Milk?' Marnie appears to be delighted that we've accepted her invitation.

The interior of this chalet is very pink. Various shades of pink fight for attention against each other in every corner of the house. There's a lot of knick-knacks in this room which makes the lounge area feel like a much smaller space than it actually is. Freya claps her hands with glee; given her love for all things pink this is basically her dream house.

We all share our drink preferences and I sit down in a flowery armchair. The whole place is outdated and appears too old-fashioned for our host. She must only be a few years older than my mum. Perhaps she inherited it from someone or purchased it like this and never got round to doing it up. Or maybe this is just her style.

The sweet tea perks me up. I notice that Leah is quieter than usual and her eyes look tired. Freya is already munching happily on a chocolate biscuit from the old-fashioned biscuit tin Marnie offered to her. She licks the crumbs from her lips and cheekily dips her hand in the tin for another.

'Make sure you ask first,' I say to my daughter, who gives me a mischievous grin in response.

'Oh, she can have as many as she wants.' Marnie gestures towards the tin. 'Go on, tuck in.'

Freya springs into action straight away, saying her thanks as she stuffs a pink wafer into her mouth.

Marnie continues her discussion with my mum about how nice the ski resort is, with Marnie sharing recommendations and tips. Leah nods along politely but I can tell by the expression on her face that she's anxious. Craig arriving like that has shaken us all.

'Just two more, that's all,' I whisper to Freya. Otherwise I know she will try and work her way through all the treats in the tin.

Leah extracts herself from the conversation with our mum and Marnie. She reaches over and steals a chocolate biscuit from the tin too, giving Freya a small conspiratorial smile as she does.

'You're both spilling crumbs everywhere,' I say to them in mock distain.

Freya giggles. I'm expecting Leah to react in the same way but instead she sighs.

Sitting next to Leah reminds me of my encounter with Lindsay last night. So when my mum lifts Freya onto her knee, I take the opportunity to talk to Leah about it.

'Look, I'm not sure how to tell you this but I met someone last night—'

'A guy?' Leah asks.

'No, not like that. It was a woman. Her name was Lindsay.'

'Lindsay?' Leah instantly frowns at this. She knows who I mean.

'Yes. She said she knew you.'

Leah blinks rapidly but doesn't say anything.

'She said you had an affair with her husband. Is that true?' I'm whispering quietly now and cursing myself for bringing this up in a stranger's house but, now we've started talking about it, the words just come tumbling out of my mouth before I can stop them.

'I had a relationship with Shane, that part is true,' Leah tells me in a measured voice. 'But he didn't share the information that he was married. Otherwise I would never have gone near him.'

'Oh, I see.'

I should've realised there was a reasonable explanation. Leah is a good person and the things Lindsay was saying about my sweet-natured sister don't add up in the cold light of day.

'Lindsay is vicious. She's made my life hell and won't leave me alone,' Leah admits, biting her lip.

I see the truth of this etched in Leah's blue eyes. Now the fug of alcohol has left my brain, it occurs to me that I perhaps divulged a few too many things about my family last night. It was also a pretty big coincidence that, of all the people in the bar, Lindsay spoke to me. Did she target me deliberately?

'Why are Lindsay and Shane at the ski resort?' I ask Leah with concern.

She doesn't look at me, instead picking at her nails. Eventually she replies in a small voice, 'Let's talk about it later.'

Leah looks miserable and I feel bad for not spotting that something was up before. I make a mental note to follow this up with her later but drop the subject for now. I drain my cup and sit uncomfortably in the chair. The room is brimming with so many things that I feel cramped and hemmed in. There's something about being in this place that's making me feel jumpy. Perhaps it's the close proximity to Erin's chalet. But there's also something about Marnie that makes me feel wary. She's just a bit *too* nice. She's cooing over Freya now and buttering my mum up with compliments. So I act on my gut instinct.

'Actually, we can't stop. Freya and I have some exploring to do.'

'Are you sure you don't want another drink and a biscuit?' Marnie peers at me over her glasses.

'Thank you but no, we've got to get going.'

Leah is perched on the edge of a dusty pink settee and looks equally keen to escape.

'Are you coming with us?' I say, throwing her the opportunity to leave as well.

'Er... I need to go back to Erin's chalet as I've left my phone there. So I'll be off now too.' Leah pulls an 'I'm sorry' face at me.

I roll my eyes. Leah's obsession with her phone is just not healthy. 'OK, well message me later and I'll let you know where we are.'

I gather my things and Leah gets up as well.

Marnie and my mum are deep in conversation again. 'Mum, I know it's snowing a lot but...' I try to signal to her that I want her to come with us by giving her a small glare, but she doesn't pick up on this.

'You go on,' Mum says, reaching for the biscuit tin. 'I think I could do with another cup of tea.'

Leah says her goodbyes and hurries out of the room. My stomach is churning and I'm not feeling great about leaving my mum here. I'm just being silly though; Marnie is perfectly friendly and it might do my mum good to just sit and have a breather for another half an hour. Seeing Craig again must've been a massive shock for her. I need to clear my head a bit too and the best way to do that is to get out in the fresh air.

I hesitate though because I want me, Mum and Leah to stick together. We need to have a proper chat about Craig's sudden appearance and decide what we're going to do next. In all honesty, I just want to book the first flight out of here and go home. I feel nervy about being so close to Erin's chalet.

I call out to Leah, but she's already gone out the door ahead of me. She doesn't turn back so I can only assume that she hasn't heard me. She crosses the path and enters Snowfall Chalet once more. She looks preoccupied and the brief information she's given to me about Lindsay and Shane is concerning. I wonder if that's the only thing that's bothering her. I hope she's going to be all right going back to Erin's chalet but, as she said, Craig turning up has nothing to do with her so in theory she can be in and out to retrieve her phone without any hassle.

Freya and I escape outdoors and follow the now familiar route towards the main hub of the ski resort. I want to escape home, and yet the thought of home also dampens my mood. Our tiny house is brimming with Jesse's belongings: his gym kit, his protein shakes, his cookbooks. I have no idea what I'm going to do with it all. His father lives in America and his mother owns a house in Scotland with her new partner, they're not a close-knit family and there are no other relatives on his side that I can pass his things on to. At some point, I'm going to have to visit Jesse or organise a call to make practical arrangements. It's not just his belongings that need sorting out, there's a whole heap of life admin that needs dealing with as well and that's even before I set the wheels in motion for our divorce.

Divorce. I never thought my marriage would end, let alone like this. Jesse and I had our difficulties, and we'd been going through a tricky patch, but I thought most of that was down to external stresses, like the pressure of my work. I never guessed that Jesse had feelings for someone else. And I never thought he would make such a colossal mistake. As soon as I start going down this line of thinking, the voice in my head begins whispering the same thing again: *You married a killer*.

Stuffing my hands into my pockets, I try to shut down the thoughts that have been taunting me, the things I imagine other people are saying about me behind my back. It's like one of those trashy magazine headlines: *My husband fell in love with my sister and murdered her husband*. It's not the sort of thing that should be happening to me, in my ordinary life. Except it is.

We arrive at the main cluster of chalets and the inviting lights of the alpine bar are twinkling at me. I'm so tempted to step inside and order a liqueur coffee – or even a vodka and Coke. But I can't. I glance down at Freya, swinging in step beside me. I've got to be strong for my daughter. Today is the day when things need to start changing for the better. Craig turning up has been a horrible jolt but I can't give in to drink. I need to formulate a plan and get Freya and me home. And when I'm back, I need to start taking control of my life – divorce, new house, new beginning.

'Do you fancy a babyccino?' I ask Freya.

'Can't I have a real coffee now I'm ten?'

I shake my head. 'No, not until you're a bit older.' Jesse's health obsessions are something positive that's rubbed off on me and this was one thing he was firm on; he didn't want Freya getting hooked on caffeine too young.

'Ohhh,' Freya protests. 'Ophelia's allowed to and she's younger than me.'

'I don't think I've seen Ophelia drinking coffee and, even if she has, the answer is still no.'

Freya falls silent but she doesn't argue any further. We order our drinks and then find some seats at a long, low wooden table with an incredible view across a side of the Alps that we haven't seen much of. The incline is much steeper on this side and we're treated to a view of some of the most experienced skiers as they gracefully weave tracks in the snow, swerving at just the right points and making their descent look effortless.

'They're awesome, aren't they?' I say to Freya, hoping she'll forget about asking questions about Craig for a bit.

She nods slowly. 'Soooo, are you going to tell me who he is then?'

Apparently, my daughter isn't so easily distracted.

'OK, so Erin's right, the man you saw earlier is technically your grandfather.'

Freya's face lights up. 'So I have got another grandfather!'

'You have, but it's not quite as simple as that, Freya. You see... he made Nana very sad. So we may not be spending a lot of time with him.'

'He made Nana sad?' Freya turns this information over in her mind. 'Well, Nana's the best so I don't want her to be sad.'

'Exactly, so it's going to take some figuring out as he turned up unexpectedly. Does that make sense?'

Freya nods her head. I'm relieved she's accepted this explanation.

'Let's go skiing then!' I drain my coffee and scrape back my chair. 'Come on.'

Freya sips the rest of her babyccino and ends up with a milk moustache. We joke about it and then make our way outside. The wind feels colder now and whips around our ears. We head towards a green ski slope, as I figure we may as well make the most of the resort while we're still here and I need to keep myself occupied. I'm itching to organise our journey back to England but I need to speak to Leah and my mum first.

Freya is standing confidently, and she already looks more comfortable in her skis than she did a few days ago. It's amazing how much quicker you can learn to ski when you're actually out here, on the mountains. It's a bit like learning a language, it's much easier to pick up when you're living it day in and day out. Freya shows me her moves, her knees are bent at just the right angle and I'm so proud to see how quickly she's picking things up. She glides slowly across the white blanket of snow.

'Go Freya!' I shout to her, as I catch her up. She may have been uncertain to begin with but Freya could be a good skier if she continued her lessons. Much better than me. I can't help thinking that, in this respect, she's more like Jesse. She's more naturally athletic than I am. I lose concentration and start to pick up pace. I jab my pointy ski poles but the lower part of my body is already slipping forward. Another skier swerves out of the way to avoid me. And then I tumble, gravity tugging me further down.

It crosses my mind, as I'm hurtling towards an inevitable accident, that my physical actions right now are mirroring my life. All it took was one short, sharp knock to make me veer off the perfect course I'd set for myself, and now I can't stop spiralling.

As I struggle to prevent myself from unceremoniously crashing into the barrier at the bottom of the slope, I squeeze my eyes shut before making impact.

But it doesn't stop the pain searing through me.

And the shame and the tears all at once overwhelm me.

When will my life stop hurting? Will I ever feel in control again?

Chapter Twenty-Two

Leah

I want to scream.

Sitting in Marnie's cluttered chalet, I'm not quite sure how I managed to keep my behaviour normal. I take in a lungful of air now that I'm back outside again.

I'm in deep shock.

Xavier is dead. *He's dead*. I saw him with my own eyes.

How? Why? Who?

There are so many questions circling in my mind. I was only with him yesterday. He was solid, he was real, he was alive. And now... he's gone.

My skin goes clammy as I think about the blood, there was so much of it. I should've called someone straight away; I should've alerted the police. But seeing another dead body terrified me. Finding Aaron lifeless at the foot of the marble staircase at Christmastime was horrific. So walking into that chalet to discover Xavier was like reliving my worst nightmare. I can't even process it right now. I need some time by myself so I can go over things properly and then decide what to do. He may have already been found. Then again, it's not midday yet and Isla and Fernando could both still be asleep after last night's party.

Xavier's features swim into my thoughts. I hadn't known him long, but I just had this feeling we'd be good together. But I can't go down that line of thinking. I can't break my heart over someone I only knew for such a short time. And perhaps I didn't know him very well at all, because someone hated him enough to kill him.

Was it Fernando? There was something about the guy that creeped me out but he and Xavier appeared to be such good friends. Maybe it was Isla? The two of them also seemed to have such a close relationship. Why would either of them want to murder him? A million possibilities crash through my mind. Had Xavier really pissed someone off so much that they went so far to end his life? Or could there be another reason for his death...

I take another deep breath in and out and gather myself for a moment before slinking back into Snowfall chalet. My plan is to creep in and grab my mobile and then escape. I want to avoid engaging in conversation with Erin if at all possible – and I'm even less keen to have any kind of exchange with Craig. What a shocker it was to see him show up. I can't believe Erin has been in touch with him. She mixes with a different class of people now but he's her father, so I suppose the pull to have him in her life was too hard to resist.

Tiptoeing down the hallway, I enter the room I've been staying in and go straight to the bedside table. My phone isn't there. I was certain I left it plugged into the charger but both the phone and the charger are nowhere to be seen. Flipping over the pillow and then the duvet cover, I rummage around in the bed to try and locate the device. I then check under the bed, in the ensuite bathroom and in the pile of clothes I was wearing yesterday. The phone has vanished.

I'm not one of those people who usually loses their phone – or anything for that matter. I'm pretty good at keeping track of everything, partly down to all the years I've spent globetrotting. So it's puzzling that my mobile is now missing as well as my cosmetics bag. Casting my mind back to a few hours ago, I was in a complete state and the events of the morning are a bit of a blur. Firstly there was the discovery of Xavier's body and secondly was the surprise arrival of Craig. The only explanation is that I took my phone with me into the open-plan, communal area.

I don't want to have to hunt around for my belongings under Erin's watchful gaze but I remind myself again that the whole situation with Craig has absolutely nothing to do with me – he's not my father. So I straighten my posture and prepare to venture into the room where I last saw Erin and Craig to check for my mobile there.

As I make my way through the chalet, I hear a distinctive noise. The opening bars of my favourite song – which also happens to be my phone ringtone. I backtrack, following the sound of the music. It leads me outside the children's room. I open the door and enter. Immediately, I see Jasper sitting in front of the TV, completely absorbed in a cartoon show. Ophelia is on her bed, her head bent over a glowing screen. She looks up at me guiltily – it's my phone.

'Ophelia!' I exclaim, putting my hand out. 'Give it back to me.'

'I was only looking...' Ophelia begins, tilting her chin in the air defiantly. She doesn't let go of the phone.

'Now.' My tone is firm as I lean towards her and grab the phone.

It's just a small metal object, so it's funny how much it means to me. But my whole life is literally on that phone. Everything from my bank details to my work contacts. I slip the cool, familiar shape into my back pocket.

Then something else catches my eye. In the middle of Ophelia's bed is a square, blush-coloured bag.

'My cosmetics!' I cry. 'Ophelia, did you take these as well?'

'I just wanted to try them out Auntie Leah,' Ophelia replies in a quiet voice.

'So you mean you've had them all along? Since yesterday?'

She nods reluctantly.

I laugh breathlessly. 'Oh Ophelia, you should've just asked me.' I'm so pleased to discover that Lindsay hadn't somehow stolen the cosmetics from my handbag or this chalet that I can't be cross with my niece.

'If you want me to do your make-up some time then just ask. I'd be happy to.'

Ophelia's eyes light up at this. 'Yes, I'd love you to!' She pauses and then says, 'I'm sorry I took it without asking.'

'Don't worry about it.'

I hug the bag to my chest. I'm glad to have found it now and to have got to the bottom of the disappearance. As well as there not being an untoward explanation, finding the cosmetics has saved me a lot of hassle. Trying to replace everything would've been costly and annoying. I make a mental note to keep a list of everything I have in there – doing an inventory could make a good video content piece as well.

I feel a pang of sorrow because I know I might not see Ophelia for a while again. I haven't decided where I'm going when I get to the airport, but I'm going to get as far away from here as possible. I may head to Thailand or Cambodia. Somewhere where I can lose myself in a different culture. I wish I could stop to do Ophelia's make up but I know I need to get going.

'I love you Ophelia,' I say with with sadness in my voice. 'And you too Jasper,' I call over to the boy who's still totally entranced in the TV programme. He doesn't move and Ophelia is giving me a weird look, so I ruffle her hair and speed out of the room.

If I give into my emotions now, I might drown in them. Finding Xavier's body in the small hours of this morning hasn't really sunk in properly yet. But it's compounded the emotions I've been experiencing since I discovered Aaron's body in December. I need to confront my feelings but first I need to get out of here.

I head back to my room and rapidly pack all my clothes back into my suitcase. I empty the bathroom of my lotions and potions before double checking I have everything. I've decided to get out of the resort as soon as I can. I don't want to become embroiled in the family argument that's brewing and I don't want to have to endure any questioning when the police arrive to find out what happened to Xavier. I can't face it.

As I'm zipping up the overflowing suitcase, my mind is again trying to work out who would want to kill Xavier, my almost-boyfriend. Isla and Fernando were closest to him so I naturally circle back to them. I try to imagine what could have caused an issue between Xavier and his friends. Or maybe his demise was an accident? I'd like to try and convince myself this is the case but I saw the knife in his flesh and the amount of blood. Whoever killed him, meant to.

Turning over likely suspects, I gasp out loud. Lindsay and Shane were at the resort last night, and they were threatening me. And then

Lindsay cosied up to Sasha. I need to get to the bottom of exactly what the conversation was between them but I really don't like the idea that Lindsay singled out my older sister and no doubt plied her with drink. But would Shane and Lindsay have killed someone close to me as a warning? To scare me? Surely they wouldn't go that far? Shane always came across as laid-back and carefree but Lindsay certainly is not and her recent behaviour has confirmed that. And they've come all the way from Australia to prove they want more from me. Is Lindsay the person responsible for Xavier's death? Or did she put Shane up to it?

My phone vibrates and I quickly check to see what the notification is. I'll need to do a thorough look through my phone – I don't know how much Ophelia was snooping around the contents.

I read the message and reread it again. I press my hand to my lips to stop myself from sobbing out loud. The social media notification I've just received makes my blood run cold. I sit down in the middle of the floor and my fingers fly over the screen. How is this happening? And why now?

Someone has hacked my social media and posted across all my platforms earlier this morning. It's a selfie of me with Shane – I'm cursing myself for not deleting it – and the caption reads:

Dear followers, here's my secret: I've been having an affair with another woman's husband.

The responses are vicious, all kinds of ridicule and hate memes have been sent my way already. My stomach drops. I always thought I had a strong community of followers – people who had my back and would fight my corner – but there are only a handful of messages suggesting I may have been hacked and even fewer voices of reason who are calling for others to wait for my next update. It's thrown my world upside down to discover that I'm just as vulnerable as any other online persona.

What do I do now?

I close my eyes and try to move past my panic. What I need is a to-do list. Firstly, I have to remove all mentions of this message as a starting point. My fingers fly across the keypad as I work to take it down immediately. Secondly, I check my emails and there's already one from my manager asking me what I'm playing at. As soon as I read it, I'm thrown off my to-do list. I feel like I'm drowning in embarrassment. How do I salvage things from here? Will anyone believe my phone was hacked? Or that I was tricked into the relationship with Shane and that I had no idea he was married? Has my reputation been tainted forever? Is this the end of everything I've worked so hard to build?

The social media post must've come from Shane or Lindsay. But how have they hacked my accounts? And is any of this linked to Xavier's death? I think back to Erin warning the pair of them off last night. What did she say? Was last night the catalyst to all this? Things have become far too complicated, far too quickly.

There must be something I'm missing... Ophelia just had my phone but she's just a child. She wouldn't have done this, would she? Would she even know how to? And how much of this has she seen? I flip back through my open tabs, but I've been updating things so speedily that I have no idea what was open when I retrieved the phone back from my niece.

Dashing back into the children's room, I find Ophelia sitting side by side with Jasper. They're both now watching TV together. Ophelia's long, red hair is flowing down her back and she's wearing powder-blue sportswear, similar to Erin's, that makes her look older than her nine years.

'Ophelia!' I call to her. 'I need to speak to you.'

Jasper doesn't even stir but Ophelia obediently follows me into the hallway. I hold up my phone. 'What were you doing when you were on my phone?'

Ophelia's pretty face looks like a picture of innocence. 'I was playing a game – the one with the little people.'

I scroll through my phone and the game she mentions is one of the open tabs. 'Did you go onto anything else, anything at all?'

Ophelia shakes her head. 'I just wanted to play the game. I'm sorry.'

My simmering anger immediately cools. My niece is just a little girl. I can't accuse her of uploading a message like that to the internet. How would she know about Shane for starters? I shake myself, this isn't her fault, it's just a coincidence that she happened to take my phone this morning.

'Thank you for your apology,' I say to her.

Ophelia hesitates. 'Can I go now?' She's already looking over her shoulder, into the room where her brother is.

Nodding, I move away, my attention back on my phone. I've had several missed calls from my manager. So I log in to my voicemail messages and listen. Unsurprisingly, he's asking me to call him straight away. The panic in his voice is blatant. He's already getting messages from brands that I have contracts with, asking what's going on. My income as well as my reputation is at stake.

I click delete at the end of the recording, not wanting to relive that message at any point. And then it clicks through to another unheard voice message, one that I hadn't clocked on my notifications.

The voice immediately startles me and then my mouth falls open. I can't believe what I'm hearing. My phone being hacked is nothing in comparison to this.

This is much, much worse.

Chapter Twenty-Three

Nadia

Craig is back. How is this possible? I'm completely gobsmacked to see him out of prison, let alone here in the French Alps. He's certainly kept his release under wraps from me and the revelation that Erin has been in contact with him for so long has rocked me. Seeing him again has thrown up so many emotions, so many fears. But I can't go to pieces because my family needs me. I'm the only one who truly knows what Craig is capable of, so I've got to be on my guard and I need to find a way to navigate us all through this, so we come out the other side – unscathed.

'Biscuit?' Marnie passes the circular tin to me. It's brimming with a mixture of chocolate biscuits and pink wafers.

I've been through a fair few rough patches in my time – my rocky relationship with Craig, raising my daughters alone, and then losing the love of my life Simon in a car accident – through it all I've always put my brave face on to the rest of the world. Because that's what strong women do, right? But, I have to admit, I'm a comfort eater. Jesse's influence kept me trim and in shape – left to my own devices I'm not sure what state my body would be in. Because when the going gets tough, my body craves sweet things to help get me through, and plenty of chocolate bars have been eaten as a result of dramas with my children, money worries or pure grief. So I dip my hand into the tin and select two of the wafers. They remind me of my own childhood and they're just what I need after the rollercoaster morning I've had.

Marnie and I make small talk. I sip my tea, only half tuned into Marnie sharing her life story with me and her love of the outdoors. I get the impression she probably regales anyone and everyone with her tales of ski seasons long past. She seems like a kind soul with a genuine joie de vivre. Listening to her talking is strangely soothing.

Then Marnie asks me about myself. I splutter my tea.

'Oh, I'm so sorry,' I exclaim.

She hands me a tissue and gives me a sympathetic smile. 'Do you want to talk about it?'

I'm about to shake my head and claim that I'm just fine but Marnie is the sort of person who puts you at ease and I find myself starting to talk about how seeing Craig has knocked me for six.

'The truth is, I'm a little bit distracted because I've just seen my ex... the father of my eldest two. I wasn't expecting to see him... here. It's shaken me up more than I thought.'

'Wow, that is a big surprise. Are you not usually in touch then, why's he here?' I can see Marnie is intrigued already.

'We have minimal contact now the girls are grown up,' I say, not wanting to lie but suddenly conscious this is Erin's neighbour. I don't want to say too much in case Erin doesn't want people knowing about her father's past.

'I think he wants to be back in the family fold.' I sigh and run my hands through my hair.

'Is it time for a second chance?' Marnie suggests.

For a split second I consider her question and then shake my head.

'No. There's too much hurt, too many wrongs. I can't forgive and forget; however much time has passed.'

My thoughts go to my lovely Simon. He was my everything. After Craig went to prison, my priority was bringing up Sasha and Erin. Simon entered my life at a time when I really wasn't looking for love, but he won me over. And his death devastated me. So it was an even bigger blow to discover that Craig had been behind the faulty car that caused Simon's accident. He organised the whole thing, pulling the strings from behind his prison bars while his contacts on the outside set everything in motion. If it hadn't been for me and my connection with Craig, Simon might still be alive. I can never forgive Craig for his jealous actions.

The memory chills me. I know what Craig is really like and how violent he can be. I can't be sitting around, eating biscuits when I have a family to protect. The thought of Craig being free scares me but I've got to do whatever it takes to make sure he doesn't ruin things for anyone else – or put them in danger. Starting with Erin. She's been taken in by him and I need her to see him for what he really is: a selfish, cold-blooded murderer.

'I best go.' Standing up, I brush a few crumbs from my lap. 'Thank you for the drink.'

'So soon?' Marnie looks disappointed, glancing between me and the window. It occurs to me that she might be hoping to strike up a friendship.

Nodding, I thank her again and make my way to the door. If things had been different, if Craig hadn't shown up, then it would've been nice to get to know Marnie. But I have to deal with the hand I've been dealt, and there's no time to waste. Because I'm sure Craig has an ulterior motive for getting close to Erin, and I can guarantee it will be to do with her vast amounts of money.

Marnie carries on speaking. I hover by the door and then open it but she's still talking and doesn't take the hint that I'm eager to get going. I'm just about to say my final goodbye when I see Leah hurtling out of Erin's cabin. She looks distraught.

'Marnie, it's been lovely, but I have to go!' I move off down the path without a backwards glance.

'Leah! Wait!' I call out to my youngest daughter.

'Mom!' She grabs my hand and pulls me down the mountainside, away from Snowfall Chalet.

My stomach flips, something's happened. Has Craig already done something awful?

'What is it? What happened?'

'Mom, I need your help.' There's an expression of pure anguish across Leah's face. 'There's something I have to tell you.'

We slow to a stop and Leah blurts out, 'It's about Xavier. He's dead.' She gulps and her voice wobbles.

'And I think I know who killed him.'

Chapter Twenty-Four

Erin

'Don't worry, I'm not going anywhere.'

I'm standing at the window, watching for any further movement from Marnie's chalet. My father's words reassure me. None of this was ever going to be plain sailing and I wasn't exactly expecting a happy family reunion, but I didn't anticipate my mother walking out on the situation so quickly. I envisioned tears and shouting but not the stubborn refusal to engage with my father at all.

'I've been playing the long game for most of my life, so I've just gotta keep playing it.'

Turning to face him, I realise he's right. There was no chance of him being accepted back into the family straight away. And we could just carry on with my father being part of my life but steering clear of everyone else's. That would be the easiest option. But I can't explain how badly I want this – a family unit involving both of my parents. I want the twins to have a relationship with both of their maternal grandparents now their father is gone. I know Aaron's father and stepmother will continue to spoil them and I'm grateful they have a positive relationship with the twins. But they're both so aloof and formal, they're not the kind of people to tell them stories or kick a football around with them.

'Chin up, Nadia will come round. I know it.' My father gives me one of his lop-sided grins. The most important thing is that he's out of prison and he's here with me. He's committed some terrible crimes in his time and got mixed up with some awful people but that all happened when he was a young man. He's told me how much he regrets it all. He's been locked up for so long and I just wanted to finally have my father free. Underneath all the bravado and the tattoos is someone who I know just wants to live out the next phase of his life with his family. He's told me this so many times, and I want him to have some happiness.

Over the years, he's shared with me information about his upbringing, the poverty his family were in, and the influence his father – a London gangster and small-time crook – had on him. He was from a background that meant if the money wasn't there, you had to steal to eat. And if someone was threatening you, you had to act because your life depended on it. I don't believe anyone is born a killer, but circumstances can force you into it. I should know.

Ophelia and Jasper cautiously make their way into the main room.

'Come in,' I smile at them. 'It's time to meet your grandfather.'

'Grandfather! Ha! That sounds a bit too posh for my liking. You can call me Pops, that's what I used to call my old granddaddy.'

'Pops!' This amuses Jasper.

I purse my lips and feel my shoulder muscles tighten. Pops is fine, but it's retro. A little bit of me is flinching at how Jasper and Ophelia referring to him as Pops might go down in their friendship circles. But, if it makes him happy, Pops it will be.

Besides, I have a whole plan to reinvent Craig Turner. I'll kit him out with the best designer clothes and teach him how to interact with the circles I move in. He's a fast learner and I'm certain he's going to make something of his golden years. There's a sharpness and intelligence to my father that could come in useful. Yes, he got caught and paid the price for it but he's told me of the number of other offences he got away with – robberies and fraud – and you never know when someone with specific skills like that might come in handy.

Jasper is the more confident of the twins right now, which isn't always the case, whereas Ophelia hangs back. I tell Jasper to make Craig a fizzy drink from the SodaStream. It was the right move, soon they're laughing at the overspill of bubbles and, before long, Jasper is chatting away animatedly and Ophelia is sitting on my father's knee. At least the children were won over easily enough.

Standing back at the window, I see my mother and Leah further down the hill. Leah has just snuck into the chalet and rushed out again. She thought I wasn't aware, but there's not much that gets past me. Besides, she hurtled outside so noisily just now that even the twins noticed.

I strain my eyes as I look out of the window. My mother and Leah are talking animatedly to each other, I can glean this from the arm gestures they're making, but they're a little too far away for me to see their facial expressions. Peering through the falling snowflakes, I see Marnie standing at her own window and she's shaking her head. I'm assuming this means Sasha is no longer with her either. I clench my jaw, frustrated. She was supposed to keep them all at her chalet for longer. The plan was for her to keep my mother and sisters with her for a little while to give them a chance to calm down. I was then going to rush over there and fake an emergency with one of the twins to get them to come back to the chalet. I'm going to have to think of something else now. I guess I can't get too annoyed at Marnie; she's been a useful ally so far. She's always more than happy to assist with anything that I ask for help with.

My father arrived at the ski resort yesterday. He went to Marnie's and stayed there overnight. She enjoyed having company and was happy to put him up. An image of Craig sitting amongst the pink cushions springs to mind and it cheers me up somewhat. But I can't dwell on it, there's work to be done. For now, I set about putting together a hearty lunch of tomato soup and thick cut bread, generously spread with butter. I've worked up an appetite after the morning's events and I know the twins will be ready for food too. As I stir the red liquid in the saucepan, I tune into the conversation my father is having with Jasper and Ophelia.

'And did you know you have another aunt and uncle as well?' my father is saying.

My ears prick up at this. I wasn't sure what to think when Craig first told me that he had two other children from another relationship: Brianna and Owen. The idea of Craig having a whole other family felt strange, but it turned out their mother had passed away some time ago and neither Brianna or Owen had any idea of where their father was. Perhaps my half-sister and half-brother will turn out to be people I have more of a connection with than my own full-blood sister, Sasha. After ten years of being estranged from my mother and the sisters I grew up with, I now seem to be craving connection with my father and the siblings I've only recently learnt of.

There are plenty of family secrets amongst the Turners and the Baileys, and they all seem to be unravelling at once.

Chapter Twenty-Five

Sasha

It hurts when you fall, but sometimes the stinging aftermath is harder to deal with than the initial pain of the incident itself. That's been the case for me following my earlier tumble on the slopes. And also true of these past few weeks following the abrupt end to my marriage and the huge disruption in my life since.

Sitting at the ski café, I've got a generous mug of hot chocolate complete with whipped cream and caramel flavouring. The rush of sugar is helping after my dramatic descent from the smallest slope in the resort. Thankfully, there's no broken bones or twisted ankles but I am feeling a little sore as a consequence. Freya had only just got out onto the snow so, rather than stop her fun, we found a ski session for her to tag onto. She's booked in for the rest of the afternoon and she can even have dinner with the other kids afterwards. She seemed happy about having some extra practice and, as I watched her out of the café window, I could see that within minutes she was chatting away with a rosy-cheeked girl her own age. I'm grateful for the respite in the nice, warm interior in the meantime.

It's also given me time to organise our escape. While I've been sitting here, I've been able to check flights and, luckily, there's a late-night departure this evening. It's not an ideal time for Freya – the plane leaves close to midnight – but it's from the closest airport and it means Freya can have a few last hours in the snow before we grab our belongings and get as far away from Craig Turner as we can. So I've sorted out the booking and I feel a bit better now that I have a plan in place. There's plenty of seats available so mum and Leah should also be able to take the same flight.

Checking my watch, I realise it's gone past lunchtime. Freya had a sandwich from her rucksack before she joined the ski session but I'm not in the mood for anything too heavy to eat. The hot chocolate is enough for me. I've got a few hours to kill and, while I could stay here gazing out at the mountain tops, I feel like I need to burn some energy before the journey home. I decide that I'll take one more trip out onto the slopes as well but, before I do so, I realise I could return to Snowfall Chalet and gather our suitcases and our bags while Freya is entertained. I spoon some of the delicious cream into my mouth and decide that retrieving our things now is the best course of action. It means Freya won't have to go back into the chalet and I can keep her away from any further awkward conversations.

Freya is now clambering onto the magic carpet ski lift, a radiant smile on her face as she ascends back up the small slope. Extracting my phone from my pocket, there's no messages from Leah and I'm worried in case something else is happening at Snowfall chalet. She was only meant to be going back there to retrieve her phone. The thought spurs me on to get back to the chalet and extract my belongings as well as my little sister so we can get out of this ski resort. I won't feel happy until I'm as far away from Craig as possible.

It's absolutely freezing when I step outside. Over the last few days I've got used to the cold weather but the temperatures feel like they have plummeted even more as I weave between the throngs of people arriving at the hub of the ski village for an afternoon of winter sports. I pass a group of teenagers, their energy levels almost palpable, as they impatiently wait their turn by the T-bar ski lift. One of them is doing little jumps in their skis and another is bouncing on their snowboard. I'm almost envious of them and their high-spirited exchanges. I wish I could turn the clock back to being that age. With the benefit of hindsight, I'd make so many different choices. But this is where I am in my path of life and there is no magic wand to wind back time. I just have to make things better going forward.

Stomping past a column of trees, I note the sparkling frost on the leaves and the magical effect it has. And then I go past chalet after chalet. There's one, right by the main road, and I can hear laughter coming from the interior before the outer door bangs shut. Glancing into the window, I see a family huddled around a fire. Two parents and two kids. The perfect, traditional family unit. They have no resemblance to the family I was raised in or the one I've created. It strikes me this is the 'norm', the family structure the rest of society wants us to achieve. I see it everywhere – in the two-adult-and-two-children-family pass to the farm, the summer holiday package deal, even the pizza family-bundle offer. I have no interest in trying to mould my life to conform to expectations, even nowadays, of what family should look like. But there's no denying the happy faces and the natural ease of this group of people is something I would love for myself and Freya.

Snowfall Chalet is in sight and, suddenly, it hits me. I acknowledge I'm struggling with having Erin back in my life. As if it wasn't hard enough being with her again after the explosive way in which she left our family a decade ago, it's been even harder to get to grips with this new dynamic knowing that, even if it was unintentional, she stole my husband's affections. That was the catalyst for his downfall and the eruption that's burnt through everything in my world since.

The heavy cloud that hung over the resort earlier today is starting to lift and the haziness of my mind is also starting to defog as well. It seems obvious now: I need to untangle myself from Erin. It's too much being in close proximity with her. We've always rubbed each other up the wrong way and now that feels amplified. It doesn't mean that I'm never going to talk to her again, it just means I need some breathing space.

Smoothing my hand across my forehead, it feels good to have the next step in place. Erin's still my sister but we're very different people. She wants to pursue building bridges with our biological father, but I have zero interest. So I need to extract myself from her orbit while she's on this track. I sincerely hope that it all goes well for her but my mum's words are ringing in my ears. I can't see that Craig is going to bring anything but trouble to Erin's door.

From the outside, Snowfall Chalet looks like all the other chalets along this cluster of buildings. Except that I know indoors the dynamics are very different to the picture-perfect family I witnessed just a little while ago. I have no idea what kind of scene I'm going to enter when I go through that bright blue front door. But I need to get this over with, so I can fly back to England with Freya. She's the most important thing to me and I don't feel safe anymore with Craig around.

'Sasha, is that you?' Erin's voice rings out as soon as I step inside. She's probably been watching from the window and knows full well that it is me.

Clearing my throat, I respond. 'Yep, it's me.'

Erin's zoned in on me, and is standing hand on hips, her body language screaming confrontation. There's no way I'm going to be able to make this a quick in-and-out by the looks of things. And, actually, it's probably best we say whatever we need to say now and get our feelings out in the open. My intention is to reiterate that I don't want Craig in my life – now or ever.

'Where did you go?' Erin demands.

'Freya and I have had a girlie morning and now she's having a ski lesson.'

I see Erin's jaw twitch. 'Shame. The twins would've liked to join her.'

Don't snap, don't snap, don't snap. My resolve to be civil and grown-up about things is challenged immediately. Erin knows exactly how to push my buttons and I swear she's doing it deliberately now.

'I wanted her to have some more skiing time... before we go.'

I skim past Erin, in an attempt to end the conversation. But, of course, it's not that easy.

'Go?' She arches her eyebrows in the way that she does when she's not happy.

'Freya and I will be flying home tonight. It's been nice staying with you and we really appreciate your invitation but you've got another guest now and we don't want to overcrowd.' I blurt all of this out quickly. I know I sound too formal but I just want to say what has to be said and go. I'm keen not to prolong things.

Erin cackles a high-pitched laugh. 'Don't be ridiculous, there's plenty of room.' She throws her arms wide as if to demonstrate exactly how much space she owns. The gesture irritates me. I think of the tiny house that I own only half of and how hard I've worked for it, putting in late nights to ensure children sit the right exams, or have adequate lunchtime provisions, or to organise a celebration for one of the school staff. In comparison, Erin married rich and has had the resources to renovate multiple properties. It doesn't seem fair and this just feels like she's rubbing it in and using her wealth to her advantage.

'Erin, it's been so kind of you but I need to go home – I need to get my head straight.'

Craig enters the room as I say this. I flush scarlet, not wanting this virtual stranger to know my business. As far as I'm concerned, he has no part in my life. Simon was the man who earned the title of father to me.

'Sasha, this is a shock. I didn't want to just turn up but I didn't believe you'd see me any other way. Am I right?' Craig's expression is earnest and there's a warmth to his voice.

He's good, I'll give him that.

My lip curls automatically. 'Correct.'

Craig chortles. 'You're your mother's child—'

'Yes, I am. And I'm proud to be.' I pause, steadying my voice and keeping it level. 'My mind won't change, I'm sorry but you don't have a place in my life.'

Craig plants his feet a little wider on the floor. He opens his mouth to reply but Erin cuts in.

'For God's sake, Sasha. Why do you have to be so stubborn about everything?'

'Me? Stubborn?' I say incredulously. This is from the person who refused to have contact with her mother and sisters for ten years.

'You've always been the same. Just give him a chance.'

'Why. Should. I.' My eyes are blazing with anger now. I'm not hanging around to continue to argue over this.

I charge through the chalet, grabbing things along the way – Freya's night-time teddy, her spare bobble hat, my scarf. Hurriedly, I bundle everything that belongs to me or my daughter into my big suitcase and chuck a few random things – toothbrushes, comb, Freya's bracelets – into my rucksack. It takes me less than ten minutes to pull everything together. Dragging the case after me, I rush towards the door.

Erin is blocking my way. 'Jasper and Ophelia are going to be so sad if Freya goes. Why don't you stay just one more night?'

'Erin, I don't want to fight. Let's talk again when we're back in England. I hope you enjoy the rest of your holiday.'

I'm really, really trying to stay in control.

'How dare you just go!' Erin screeches at me, losing her temper first.

'This isn't about you, Erin,' I shout back. 'Just let me out the chalet.'

She rages, hurling accusations at me. 'After everything you've done, you could at least attempt to be civil to our father.'

I look at her aghast. 'What do you mean? What have I done?'

'Oh don't play dumb Sasha!' Erin folds her arms across her chest and arches her eyebrow in that way she does.

'No, tell me, what have I done?'

'It was because of you that I had to leave all those years ago!'

I shake my head in disbelief. 'Really Erin? Because that's not how I remember it. You stormed off when things got hard and then you turned your back on us all.'

'What! So you didn't push me out with your constant jibes? I felt guilty enough about what happened to Leah as it was, but the way you went on at me... it was cruel.'

I roll my eyes. I'm stunned she's pinning so much of this on me. From my recollections, everyone was mad at her for what she'd done.

'And that's before we even get into the matter of Jesse —' Erin's face is alight with fury as she spits these words at me.

I throw my hands up. 'I'm not listening to this!' Honestly, I didn't think she'd go there but she has.

'Stop,' Craig intervenes. 'You two need to sit down and talk this out.'

'I don't have to do anything.' I shoulder past Erin and out the door, balancing the rucksack and the suitcase as I go. She's still shouting accusations at me, but I've blocked out her words. I was a fool to think we could salvage our relationship.

Hurrying away from the chalet, the snow feels slippery underfoot. So my focus is on putting one foot in front of the other and staying upright. I don't want another fall.

Out the corner of my eye, I catch Marnie staring out of her window at me. It's unnerving that she always seems to be watching.

I think I hear footsteps behind me but I don't turn to look back. I just keep going, away from the chalet. My leg is still a little sore but I'm going to have one last ski on the slopes to clear my head, then I'm on the first plane out of here. I need to get back to England to sort my life out.

I can't stay here any longer, not with Craig at the chalet. I have to put some distance between me and my messed-up family.

Chapter Twenty-Six

Leah

'Listen to this.' I check the pathway we're standing on and there's no one else in sight. So I click play on the voicemail message and switch to speakerphone so Mom can hear it too.

There's some muffled noises and then Xavier's voice can be heard. I can't decipher exactly what he's saying at first but then one word stands out – loud and clear. Xavier unmistakably says 'Erin'. There's movement and then the sound of the voice recording going dead.

Mom's hands fly to her face. 'Is there any more?' she whispers, her expression horror-struck.

I shake my head slowly. 'That's it.'

We both fall silent. I'm convinced this means that Erin was there last night when Xavier was killed. And there's more.

'There's a message from Xavier, he texted me not long after I left his chalet.'

Mom takes the device from me and reads out the words:

Call me, Leah. It's about Erin. You need to know that she killed Aaron. Call me urgently.

Mom starts to shake and almost drops the phone.

'Whoa.'

And then it all clicks. The expression on Mom's face says everything.

'You knew!' I exclaim.

'I...'

'You knew she killed Aaron, didn't you? How could you keep that a secret? Why haven't you gone to the police?' My voice is getting more hysterical. This can't be real. There's so many secrets and they're all twisting into one big web of lies.

'Sshhhh!' Mom grips my wrist. 'Keep your voice down.'

'Oh my God! Is this true?'

'Leah, listen to me. There are reasons.'

My heart plummets, I don't know if I want to know the full extent of what's been going on. Maybe I'm better off in blissful ignorance.

'You can't say *anything*.' My mother's voice is low and tinged with a desperation I've never heard from her before.

I'm sick of all the family secrets. Why can't things be more straightforward? I'm regretting coming back from Australia now. Yes, things are complicated with Shane. But I've jumped from the frying pan into the fire.

'Mom, if Erin has killed her own husband and if she's behind Xavier's death too then... then we must go to the police. She's dangerous.'

My mom mutters something under her breath, but the wind carries her words in the opposite direction. Her teeth are chattering and I realise just how much colder it is now in comparison to yesterday.

'Let's get inside and I'll explain.'

Mom guides me towards the building that leads to the chair lifts. It's quiet over this side of the mountain at this time of day. Instead of going to the counters to buy tickets for the chair lifts, Mom steers me towards the other end of the L-shaped room. There are a few sofas, a couple of vending machines, a carousel of tourist leaflets and a bookcase full of second-hand paperbacks. To me, this area looks like a square of the ski resort they forgot in the recent renovations. Everywhere else has plush furnishings and carefully thought-out designs. This tiny section gives a glimpse of what the ski resort might have looked like in its nineties heyday, all shabby-chic and tons of wood panelling.

Sinking into the soft cushions of the old sofa, I pinch the bridge of my nose and brace myself for whatever my mom has to tell me.

'Leah, I admit, I knew Erin was involved in Aaron's death. The thing is, she put Jesse up to it.'

'What?' This makes no sense. Jesse hadn't seen Erin for years, and he had Freya and Sasha. 'Why?'

Mom gives me a knowing look.

'He was more than infatuated?' Exasperated, I hit the arm of the sofa with the flat palm of my hand. 'Of all people, Jesse...'

'I know... I think the connection Jesse and Erin have is complicated.'

'Say no more, please.' Jesse having an affair is bad enough but Erin being the person he was cheating with is too much.

I turn over the conversations and events in my head. 'So Xavier somehow found out Erin was involved in Aaron's death?'

'I'm afraid I don't know the answer to that one.'

'But Erin must have found out and then killed Xavier because of what he knew.'

Mom looks down, hands clenched tight around each other. 'We don't know that.'

'Oh, come on. You heard the voicemail.'

'You're jumping to conclusions,' Mom says with force, holding my gaze now. 'I haven't told a soul about Erin's part in what happened at the Christmas party. And you're not going to either.'

'How can I—'

'We're family, she's your sister. That's enough. I'd do the same for you.'

Her words hang heavily in the air between us. A sickening sensation of unease rises in my throat and I can't find the words to respond. I don't want there to be any more secrets but the consequences would be colossal. Mom would never forgive me. The twins would lose their mother after just losing their father. And where's the evidence? Erin's got away with things so far and she'd hire the best lawyers to fight against the truth.

Mom's words niggle at me as well because, until my dealings with Shane and Lindsay, I'd always been quite clear in my views of right and wrong. I'd have said I have a strong moral compass. But Shane's deception has been my undoing. As a result of someone else's dishonesty, I ended up panicking and making a grave error in my judgement. I shouldn't have sent money to them to try and buy their silence – especially when I'd done nothing to be ashamed of. I've learnt that sometimes things aren't as clear cut as they seem.

'Erin had a difficult relationship with Aaron, and she didn't have our support during their marriage. I feel guilty... if I'd been there for her then maybe her actions wouldn't have been so drastic. Maybe I could've helped her...' Tears spring in Mom's eyes.

My shoulders sag. I'm starting to see where my mom is coming from. There's always another side to the story. It's true when they say you never know what you'd do or how you'd feel until you experience a situation yourself. You have to walk in another person's shoes before you can pass judgement. Even if the thing they've done is the worst thing imaginable.

'I won't say anything.'

'Thank you.' Mom reaches over and pats my hand. 'Let's go up in the ski lift then. I'm keen to see the view from up there. We'll go back to Snowfall Chalet in a bit, and we can sort things out then. First, I think we need a breath of fresh air.'

'You can't get fresher than here,' I joke weakly.

Mom gets up and heads towards the ticket office. Thoughts jumble and blur together. My mother has carried on as though nothing is wrong but she's had a long time to think about all of this whereas I'm still reeling from the most shocking conversation of my life.

And then my phone rings.

It's another unknown number. Instead of ignoring it, this time I pick up.

'Who is this?'

Silence.

'Is it you, Lindsay?'

There's a peal of laughter. 'Who else?'

It's her. My blood boils. 'You hacked my phone, didn't you?'

'No comment,' comes the response down the line. But I can tell, it was her.

'Why are you trying to ruin my life?'

'Because you ruined mine,' Lindsay bounces back at me.

'I'm sorry Lindsay, I genuinely had no idea that Shane was married. Please sort this out between the two of you and leave me alone.' I take a deep breath. I don't believe Lindsay and Shane had a happy marriage before his relationship with me. Or that it was the first time he cheated. But Lindsay is determined to blame her marital troubles on me.

I end the call. I don't expect that will be the last I hear from her and my suspicions about the phone hacking being down to Lindsay seem to be confirmed. At least it wasn't anything to do with Ophelia.

A wave of exhaustion sweeps over me. I'm done with this trip now.

I need to distance myself before the police start investigating Xavier's murder. If Erin is responsible, they may question if I – as her sister – had anything to do with it. Or they could pinpoint me as one of the last people to see Xavier or — even worse — the person who found his body a few hours ago and didn't report it. A sliver of fear runs through me.

I need to get out of here, before it's too late.

And before something else happens.

Chapter Twenty-Seven

Nadia

'There's another thing that's been playing on my mind.' I'm not sure how to convey this but, after the conversation I've just had with Leah, there's one last thing that needs to be said.

The sun is glowing orange and casting burning tentacles across the dusky evening sky, contrasting with the white ice-tops of the mountains. The world looks like it's on fire from up here, as I stare across the landscape from my vantage point on the chair lift. Leah is sitting by my side and our arms are linked through one another's.

Leah draws a shaky breath. It's been a lot for her to take in but I trust her.

'The timing… the timing of Xavier's… what happened to him. Well, Craig had just arrived at the ski resort.'

I let my words sink in and then look out of the corner of my eye to gauge Leah's reaction.

She sits up straighter, grasping onto the metal bar across our laps. 'I guess it's possible he had something to do with it.' She looks at me for a beat and then says, 'Are you planning to ask Erin what happened? If she was responsible?'

I wring my hands together. 'I think it's best left. What you don't know, you don't know.'

'I have to know, otherwise I'll always think it was her.' There's an insistent note to Leah's reply.

'I understand that but the alternative is that if Erin tells you the truth then you'll have that weighing on you forever. And if you were to be questioned by the police, then you can honestly say you haven't spoken to her about it.'

Leah shuffles awkwardly in her seat, causing the chair lift to rock with her movement.

'Careful!' The alarm in my voice is evident.

'These things are so sturdy Mom, it's fine.'

The view is just extraordinary but the height does make me a little nervous. There's a sheer drop below us and we're climbing higher and higher with each passing second.

'Leah, I think you should go back to Australia. Or maybe somewhere new. I don't want you to, it's been so lovely having you around, but it's better you're far away from this. It isn't your mess to get caught up in.'

My youngest daughter nods in agreement. 'I was thinking the same thing.'

'Oh, I hate to see you go.'

'You could come with me?'

'I have to be around for Erin this time.'

My eyes dampen. I'm forever torn between my three girls. I never feel like I'm sharing myself equally amongst them. It's like a constant ever-changing juggling act, where I have to keep switching my attention. The challenge is to guess which one of them needs me the most so I can try and catch them before they fall. I haven't always been successful in averting disaster but I've done everything in my power to protect my children. Fleetingly, I wonder how mothers of four or more children do it. How do they manage to stretch themselves fairly across the demands of their offspring? And will I ever get to a point where I feel like I'm getting it right?

When my children were younger, they were at least all under one roof. In some ways that was easier. Their needs were simpler then: food, sleep, schoolwork, movie marathons. In adulthood, their lives have been studded with more complex issues. It's been harder to find the answers they need and the right course of action. Some may say that I've meddled too much, but I can't help myself. However old they get, they're still my babies.

I squeeze Leah's hand. 'It'll all work out in the end.' I brush away a tear. I hate the thought of being across the other side of the world to my darling Leah once again. But it's best if she extracts herself now. She's still young and she loves to travel. There are plenty more places for her to see and experiences for her to have. I want her to be free and to live her life to the full. I don't want her to be dragged down by the choices Erin and Sasha have made.

The chair lift changes direction and begins its descent. I lose myself in the scenery once more and I'm marvelling at just how far I can see, when something snags my attention.

A mass of curly, dark hair and a purposeful stride. 'Look, it's Sasha.' I point towards the figure coming out of one of the buildings. I know it's her because of the distinctive yellow ski jacket she's wearing.

'That's the rental place,' Leah comments. 'She looks like she's hitting the slopes.'

I remember now, the building Sasha is exiting is indeed the ski hire centre. There's no sign of Freya with her and I question why she's by herself. We watch as Sasha puts on her skis and then heads towards a ski lift on one of the green slopes.

'Oh, there's Erin!' Leah says, waving her hand towards another familiar outline. Erin's red hair is unmistakable and her pale blue snowsuit also marks her out in a sea of white, green and purple ski wear. She heads in the same direction as Sasha.

'It's good to see them heading out on the slopes together,' Leah comments uncertainly.

If there's anything I know about my two eldest daughters, it's that they're both as stubborn as each other. I'm more likely to find a pot of gold at the end of the rainbow than the pair of them are to put their differences aside so soon after Craig's arrival. The idea of them clearing the air so quickly doesn't seem plausible to me.

The chair lift is nearing the ground now. I keep my eyes on Erin; she's got some skis with her too and she's following Sasha.

Something isn't adding up. I can't put my finger on why, but my guts twist with terror.

I've got a very, very bad feeling about this.

Chapter Twenty-Eight

Erin

She hasn't even noticed me. Sasha is so preoccupied with whatever's going on in her head that she hasn't even got the faintest inkling that I've been following her. Pure anger propelled me out of the chalet and after my elder sister. I hate the way she spoke to me – her tone of voice, her expression, everything about the exchange we just had fuelled my intense dislike for her even more. As if I didn't have enough reasons to want to get rid of her, and then she goes and adds another.

I'm fuming because she point-blank refused to even hear our father out. She acts so high and mighty but she forgets that we all know her flaws – the drinking, the forgetfulness, the meltdowns. My nostrils flare as I mentally tick off the many different times in which Sasha and I have clashed over the years and the frequent number of those occasions in which she's come out on top.

She won't win again. This is it now. It's my turn to be the winner. I want revenge for everything that's gone wrong in my life, because Sasha has been behind most of those moments.

Digging my nails into the soft flesh of my palms, I urge myself to act as normally as I can. I don't want anyone to look in my face and see murder in my eyes. Sasha goes to the luggage desk in the ski village to store her belongings away. I'm curious to see what she will do next.

And I'm surprised to watch her going to collect some hire skis. I got the impression she wasn't faring too well on the slopes. Then again, the lure of the mountains is strong.

Somehow, I get through the rigmarole of acquiring a set of hire skis as well. My own are back at the chalet. As I adjust them, it's clear to me how clunky they are. Not like my own high-end and customised set. But these will have to do for now. I'm sure they'll fulfil their purpose.

Forcing myself to slow down, I decrease my pace and allow Sasha time to get onto the ski lift. My brain is racing, snapshots of the past flashing into my mind's eye. I know what to do now. The small hairs on my arms are standing on end, every part of my body focused on what must happen next, thrusting me towards the inevitable moment when I face Sasha for one final showdown.

After what feels like an agonising wait, I'm being lifted up, up, up through the sky. Whenever I'm on a ski lift, it gives me the sensation I'm flying. I want to throw my arms wide and pretend to be soaring upwards, like an elegant and powerful eagle. But I stop myself. I can't draw attention now. Not when I'm so close. Not when the end is in sight.

As I predicted, Sasha has faffed around once she's disengaged from the ski lift. I witness her take a swig from her water bottle. I know the container doesn't have water in it because I've seen her fill it up with vodka and lemonade in the morning's when she thinks that no one is looking. Sasha's only just ahead of me now, she's standing just a short distance from the ski lift as I reach the top. If I called out she would hear me. But I don't, it's not time yet. I can't pounce until everything has been lined up perfectly.

Sasha's dark ski helmet gleams in the fading light of the day. The dying rays of the sun cast across her still figure and it almost looks as though she has a halo encircling her head. She always wanted to be an angel. It was her favourite pretence as a child. She always got picked to be the angel in school plays and it was her go-to outfit at Halloween too. I can picture those battered angel wings in our old dressing-up box. Then, as an adult, she always had to be the goody-two-shoes. She went from teacher's pet to assistant head, after all. Before today is done, she'll become an angel for the very last time.

Sasha adjusts her skis and tests out her ski poles. Not once has she looked around. If she did, then she'd see me for certain now. I'm so close.

Finally, she pushes off. For the briefest second, I watch her rush down the mountainside before I allow my yearning muscles to snap into action. And then I'm off, racing after her.

It doesn't take long for me to pull level with her. It's then I roar her name.

She startles but remains upright, back straight and knees bent. It's hard to see her reaction beneath her ski visor.

Before she's able to react, I swerve in front of her and she's forced to move sharply to the left. My plan is working.

I know these mountains like the back of my hand.

I know every twist and turn on the slopes.

I know where's safe and where's not.

And I know which way we're going next.

Chapter Twenty-Nine

Sasha

A figure cuts straight across my downward path and I think I hear a muffled shout of my name. I just about manage to change my course and avoid a collision. My breath catches in my throat. That was a near miss but at least I managed to avoid an accident. But now I'm veering off to the left of the run and travelling at such a diagonal angle that it's going to be impossible to get back onto the designated slope.

The sun is setting, flashing a vivid and angry orange across the sky, and I notice there are dark, heavy storm clouds on the horizon. Nature is reflecting my internal emotions. I struggle to slow down as the section I'm on is much steeper than the safe, green run I'd selected.

Briefly looking back over my shoulder, I'm aware the run isn't very busy at all and there's only a couple of other people on the slope, all concentrating on what they're doing. I doubt anyone has noticed my encounter with the rogue skier or that I'm zooming away from the well-used route and into an unregulated area.

I tell myself not to panic, my descent is likely to take me down to the bottom of the mountain and I'll probably end up near to the main hub of the ski resort. All I need to do is keep calm and in control of my skis.

Just as I'm thinking this, I'm aware of another skier coming up alongside me. I exhale with relief, assuming it must be an instructor or someone coming to help guide me back to the green run. But it must be the same person who knocked me off course a few minutes ago because the same thing is happening once more, the skier is slashing across my path and forcing me to go further left again.

'Back off!' I cry, my voice crackling with annoyance. I don't know what they're playing at.

And then it happens again.

This time, I almost lose my balance as I cut a jagged path in the snow. Trying not to be shunted in the direction they're wanting me to go but still finding myself a lot further away from the main slopes than I'm comfortable with.

Now the other person is on me, they're chasing me down, driving me further and further along the mountainside until we're on a sharp, steep decline. I've never been on a black run before but this is what I imagine it must be like. I don't have the skill to handle this and my leg is throbbing even more.

I try to assess the landscape for help but there's no one else around and the snow is starting to fall more heavily, the dark rolling clouds upon us all of a sudden. I have no idea who this person is or what they want, because I haven't been able to get a proper look at them. I'm numb with fear as they chase me through the wintery scenery.

'Stop!' I scream. 'Leave me alone!'

This only encourages them further. There's not a lot of space between us now. I look to the side and it's then I notice the pale blue ski suit. I'm astounded to see that my tormentor is known to me.

It's Erin.

My mind fills with possibilities, trying to make sense of what this means. We argued and she's followed me. She's still angry. This is not good.

And then the inevitable happens: we collide.

I go down first but my skis take her to the ground with me. We become one as we crash to the ground, meshed in our fall, hard to see where one begins and the other ends. A pain sears through my back as I land awkwardly. Erin clatters inches from me, her skis coming down on my legs with a thud. I yelp in pain.

'What are you doing?' I shout, turning on my side to confront her.

Erin rolls away from me, slithering out of her skis. For a second, I think that's it. She's made her point and she's going to leave me now. I disengage from the boards, kicking my boots free. As I stand up, Erin turns to face me. A strand of copper-coloured hair escapes her helmet and, bizarrely, I want to reach out and tuck it back in place. The instinct of an older sister.

The expression on her face is unreadable. Before I know it, she's on top of me. Throwing her weight at me and shoving me back down in clean, unmarked snow.

'Erin!'

She straddles me and grabs my wrists and her face now clouds with emotions: anger, hatred, determination.

We're out here on the mountainside all alone. Why would she do that? Why would she choose to pursue me and attack me in such a targeted way? How scared should I be?

We grapple and an image of Freya flashes through my mind. The thought of my little girl and my urge to get back to her, to get back to safety, gives me a rush of adrenaline and I manage to put enough momentum behind my actions that Erin topples off me. Landing on her back in the snow, breathless and seething with rage.

Terrified, I scramble to my feet and attempt to run. The snow is thick, my boots are heavy and it's like wading through pure white mud.

'Oh no you don't.' Erin pulls me around by my shoulder. Her teeth are gritted and she looks more frightening than I've ever seen her before.

'Erin, please.' I try to reason with her. 'This is madness.'

I put out my hands, palms held up flat to her to signal peace. She ignores me and grasps my gloved fingers and then she proceeds to yank me alongside her. I find myself being dragged in another direction. I try to resist but Erin is stronger than me.

I'm hyper aware that I'm very much alone out here with my sister. There's not another soul in sight. There's certainly no one to hear my screams, and no one to know that I'm here. This time, I can't loosen Erin's iron grip. And I'm tired, my whole body is tender from skiing, from falling, and my energy levels are starting to dip. I must stay alert but the intense cold is creeping into my bones and fear is twisting in my mind. I need to figure out how to get away from her but I don't know how.

'Here we are.' Erin cackles manically at me. 'Just the spot.'

I shake my head, trying to dislodge some of the snowflakes that have settled on my visor and are obscuring my vision. Erin lets go of me for a second and I wipe an arm across my face. I can see a little more now... even though I wish that wasn't the case.

Erin's plan is now revealed. She's been herding me towards the edge of the mountaintop. There's a sheer drop only metres away from us. Her intent is unmistakeable.

'Erin, don't do this.' My voice is barely audible but she can still hear me.

'Give me one good reason.'

'You won't get away with it.'

'Won't I?' Erin's voice is teasing. 'Where are the witnesses?' She flings an arm out to demonstrate her meaning. 'There's no one else here, it's just you and me. And no one knows I'm here. When you fall off this cliff, if they find you, they'll probably detect the alcohol levels in your bloodstream and the cause will be accidental death.'

When. She said *when* and not if. My own sister is planning to kill me and everything she's said is correct. My husband has been outed as a murderer, my life is a mess, I've been drinking a lot. It's not too much of a leap to believe that it's all been too much for me and therefore I've taken drastic measures.

I've got to try and fight back. 'There's something you're forgetting, Erin.'

'I don't think there is?'

My voice trembles but I press on. 'Your husband has just died. My husband was responsible. Who do you think the police will want to question first?'

Erin goes completely still.

'You of course. It's a classic case of revenge.'

She doesn't respond.

'If you're certain that you've not been caught on CCTV coming from your chalet to the slopes, then I agree you might get away with it. But have you thought of everything? Covered all bases? Because if you haven't, you're going to find yourself in the cell right next to Jesse.'

Erin cackles. 'You still haven't worked it out, have you? Poor, naive Sasha.' She laughs again.

My skin prickles, I don't like the turn this conversation is taking.

'Jesse pushed Aaron, that's true. But I told him to. He did it for me, because we were having an affair.'

Her words are like a punch to my stomach. She's right – I had no idea whatsoever. Her revelation has made my mind spin. I'm dizzy with the truth. Both my husband and my sister were lying to me.

'Don't think that was just a one off either.'

'What do you mean?'

The next thing she says takes my breath away.

'Aaron isn't the only person I've murdered.'

'Erin? What are you saying?'

Erin's eyes glitter with menace. 'I don't have to tell *you* any more. Just know that I am going to do this.'

My brain is scrambled. Is she telling the truth? Who else has she killed?

While I'm still making sense of her words, Erin is advancing towards me. My heartbeat slows. Reflexively, I step backwards. I know the drop is just behind me but I can't stop myself.

When she pushes me, I'm not ready for the force.

I lose my footing. The ground has given out, there's no longer anything beneath me.

Gravity pulls me down.

Chapter Thirty

Nadia

I'm too late.

I raced to the green slope and, while I was making the agonisingly slow ascent, I saw two figures darting off into the fading light. I just knew it was my eldest daughters. There was no question of what I would do next; I went after them. Using every ounce of my energy to push me towards the two figures blurred by the falling snow. I was thankful for the fact I'd kept my regular ski lessons up and I could do this. Although, it's very different being on real snow. I found myself stuck for a few minutes and it took a while to get going. Keeping track of the pair of them wasn't easy. With the light fading and the weather becoming stormier, visibility has been reduced. But I haven't let them out of my sight.

I saw the two people collide and it gave me a chance to catch up with them. It was then I noticed the cliff edge and cottoned on to Erin's plan. I've never moved so fast in my life, every muscle in my body spurring me forward.

But it's too late.

Sasha has just disappeared over the edge, right before my eyes. One second she was there and the next she wasn't.

And she's taken Erin with her.

Sasha clasped onto Erin's arm and the two of them went tumbling into the abyss.

'Nooooo!'

I pull to an abrupt stop a few steps from where my daughters were just standing. My heart is already cracking in two.

'Sasha! Erin!'

I'm scared to get too close, scared to look over the edge and witness them plummeting.

'Mum!'

The word is music to my ears. But did I really hear my daughter's voice, or am I imagining it? Cautiously I step forward and look down.

'Mum!' It's Sasha. Miracle of miracles, she's caught hold of a jutting piece of rock, slippery with ice and her feet seem to have found a foothold. The infinite depths below her make my mouth go dry. We're so high up that the ground isn't even in sight.

Sasha's face is colourless as she repeats my name for the third time. What shocks me more is that Erin is dangling next to her. Somehow, they're holding onto each other, but Erin is at a lower point to Sasha.

'I'm so sorry!' The desperation in Erin's voice makes me feel nauseous.

She's put all of our lives in danger. All three of us could end up falling through the air to our deaths. An apology is almost laughable right now but at least she had it in her to say it. I can't allow my emotions to distract me though. It's up to me to save them.

I lightly press the ground I'm standing on with my foot to make sure it's solid enough and then I slither to my belly, throw off my gloves and reach down. My fingers close around Sasha's hand, I'm holding onto her tighter than I've held onto anything ever before.

'I've got you,' I tell her.

'Don't let me go,' Sasha sobs.

'Keep calm,' I order.

There's no one else here. It's down to me, I have to save them and the only way I can do that is by keeping my wits about me.

'Mum!' Erin cries up to me. Her beautiful face etched with horror. I drink her in, wishing she hadn't done this. Wishing this wasn't happening.

And then everything happens at once. Sasha slips, her foot losing its place on the cliff-face. I use every fibre of my body to pull her up, pull her over the edge and back to me.

'Don't let go of Erin's hand,' I urge her.

Sasha's body is half over the precipice. All it takes is one incorrect move and I've lost them both forever.

And then the screaming fills my ears.

Chapter Thirty-One

Sasha

I can't stop shaking. I'm still here. I'm still breathing. I'm not dead – yet.

Going over the edge of that mountainside was the most frightening thing I've ever experienced. My levels of fear were indescribable. But, in the split second when my foot slipped, I knew exactly what was happening and my survival instincts kicked in. I managed to bend my body forward and grab hold of whatever I could to keep me from falling. If there hadn't been a ledge at that particular spot then I wouldn't be here now. Gravity would've pulled me to my death.

I break out in a cold sweat and my shaking intensifies. My mum crushes me to her as she swiftly moves me away from the edge.

'Sasha, I've got you. I've got you. It's going to be OK.' My mum soothes me with her voice as she helps me to move clear from the deadly drop.

It all happened so quickly. I behaved instinctively and when Erin pushed me I clutched onto her hand. I had hoped that holding onto her would save me. That being tethered to her would stop me falling and that she'd draw us both back to safety. But I was mistaken. Erin was so intent on pushing me that she didn't react fast enough. She ended up going over the edge too. She nearly pulled me down with her weight but for some reason I kept on holding her hand. We both managed to land on the ledge and cling onto the jagged mountain. I'll never forget the way Erin screamed. It ripped through my core.

When my mum's voice floated down to us, it was like a lifeline. A miracle. I wasn't sure how long we'd be able to stay clutching onto the side before the ground shifted beneath us or the wind whipped us to our deaths. I'm not sure I would've had the strength to climb up to safety by myself. If my mum hadn't appeared when she did, I know I would've died today.

Erin sobbing she was sorry was typical of her. Trying to save her own skin again. But she hunted me down and herded me off that edge in a chilling, premeditated way. She'd planned that and she nearly succeeded in killing me. There's no way I'm ever going to forgive her for that.

So when my mum started to haul me up after those petrifying minutes of hanging on for dear life, I'd already decided that I didn't want to risk either of us reaching back down for Erin. Who knows what Erin might have done? There was every chance she might pull my mum over the edge. Or that she'd be given another chance at life and continue down the path she's on. I couldn't risk her coming after me again or murdering someone else. Too much damage had been done by her.

So as my body slithered up the mountainside, I gave a good hard kick.

It connected with Erin's head at the same time I let go of her hand.

I didn't need to look back to know that my aim had worked.

Erin was freefalling through the sky.

After everything that's happened, she deserved it.

Erin made it a choice between my life or hers. And she almost won. I take in a long, shuddering breath.

Never in my wildest nightmares would I have wanted Erin to die like this. We had our issues but she was my sister. I was trying to rebuild my relationship with her. All this happened because of Erin's actions. She started all of this and the outcome could've been very different. She was plotting to get away with what she'd done. There's no doubt in my mind she would've walked away with a smile on her face, pretending not to know anything, and then put a comforting arm around my weeping daughter when I couldn't be found.

My mum and I stop short when we reach the abandoned skis. It feels like an age since Erin and I collided, but it probably wasn't more than half an hour ago.

My mum drops to her knees now. I crouch down beside her. She's crying quietly.

'It's all my fault.'

'No, it isn't,' I say emphatically. 'This is all of Erin's doing.'

'I was going to reach for her next.'

'I know you were. And she knew it too.'

'I thought she'd keep holding on.'

'Me too.' The first flicker of guilt snakes up my spine. If I hadn't kicked out, would Erin be with us now? If I hadn't let go of her hand? It's better to block it out, to not say anything. I can't change it now, it's done.

It's so, so cold and I can see my mum's tears freezing to her face.

'Come on, we need to get back.' I have to take charge. If Mum goes to bits, then we might both get stuck out here. The snow is falling at an ever-quickening rate and we need to find our way back to safety.

She pulls herself together and looks one last time towards the spot where she last saw Erin's face before turning to me. She puts a hand to my cheek. 'Let's get these skis on and get you back.'

We embrace briefly and then help each other to clamber into the skis. The last of my energy is ebbing away but I have to do this final push to get back to the ski resort – and to my daughter. The image of Freya in my mind has kept me going throughout the whole terrifying experience. The urge to hold my little girl in my arms – she's my reason for living. The idea of her losing me with Jesse in prison made my resolve burn bright. I don't want her to have to bury her mother in the same month her father received his prison sentence. And it's not over yet, there's still a way to go before we reach safety.

I lean heavily on my ski poles and we move slowly in the direction we came from. It was only a short while ago I was last here but in that time period Erin has fallen off the edge of a cliff. Every time I glide a little too far from my mum, panic rises in me. We can't lose sight of each other. I'm scared we will get lost out here in the snowstorm.

My teeth chatter and my eyes sting with unshed tears. But I keep my gaze trained on my mum, who's just in front of me.

I think of the safe, warm ski resort; I think of the hot chocolate with cream I was drinking just hours ago; and I think of my daughter waiting for me to pick her up after her ski session.

And I pray that we can get back through the ice and the wind and the snow.

I pray we can make it back alive.

Chapter Thirty-Two

Nadia

Blinking away the tears, my mind and body are frozen with grief. Sasha is here, beside me. It took forever, but we inched our way back to the green run. The snowfall is so bad there's been a weather warning. Staff at the ski resort spotted us stumbling down the slopes and assisted us in the final part of our journey.

Sitting with my hands wrapped around a boiling mug of coffee, I'm dazed. Medical staff at the ski centre checked us over and declared we hadn't done any lasting damage. Neither Sasha nor I mentioned that three of us left the slopes and only two came back.

Staring out across the mountain, I can't believe Erin pursued Sasha in the way she did. I saw it with my own eyes, I saw the ruthless way in which she kept steering Sasha further and further away from the resort, towards the steep, slippery edge of the mountain.

Sasha is sitting beside me and I place my hand on top of hers. Her head is bent, and she's lost in thought. My heart contracts when I think that she was almost lost to me. I take in her mane of curly, dark hair and her familiar profile. Sasha is my first-born and I've been so worried about her lately. She's the daughter who never left; she's stayed living close by to me throughout all of her adult years and she's the person I see day in and day out. Losing her would've turned my world upside down and broken me. We do everything together: the weekly shop, Sunday roasts, trips out with Freya. I don't know how I managed to pull her back from the brink; it must've been the pure strength of a mother's love.

But Erin's screams are still ringing in my ears. I didn't intentionally reach for Sasha first. She was just in the highest position and I'd watched Erin driving Sasha to this fate. Erin had put them both in danger so, given the circumstances, it was natural for me to reach for Sasha's hand first. I was going to haul Erin up next – I wanted to stop her falling too. For a brief few seconds, I thought it was possible to save both my children.

I can't believe Erin is gone.

Your children dying before you is something that no parent should ever have to go through. Erin's final moments will haunt me forever and I know I'm never going to be able to get past the question of whether I could've done something more, something different to change the outcome. Because whatever Erin had done, she was still my little girl. I still loved her unconditionally, despite her behaviour. A memory of her dancing centre stage in a school show floats into my brain. Her copper hair in a long, intricate plait and her green eyes shining with pride as she confidently moved to the music. What happened to my child?

I take a gulp of my coffee and welcome the burning feeling as the hot liquid slides down my throat. I'm numb all over so the sensation of the heat jolts me out of my thoughts and back to the present. The time is ticking on, so we can't stay here indefinitely. There are things that need to be done.

'Sasha, we need to go and collect Freya soon. Are you ready, or would you just like me to go?'

Sasha unfurls herself from her hunched-over position. There's a dazed expression on her face and I know she's experiencing similar feelings to me.

'I'll come with you,' she replies softly.

Sasha and I have already had a whispered exchange and decided that neither of us are going to tell the rest of the family, the police or anyone else what really happened to Erin. We're going to say the last we knew Erin was going skiing but she went in a different direction to us. This will tally with her hiring skis. Apart from that we're going to feign ignorance.

It means another family secret but it's a necessity. Erin kicked off the chain of events over the last ten years by instigating the affair with Jesse. Today that has ended. Truth be told, I also can't bring myself to tell Jasper and Ophelia that I witnessed Erin's plummet to her death. And I don't want to have to admit to anyone that I was forced to choose which child to reach for first.

Sasha and I make our way towards the restaurant that's the designated pick up spot for Freya. At least she'll be fed and watered and none the wiser to anything that's happened this afternoon. As we reach the entrance, I hear a voice I recognise straight away.

'Mom!' Leah is calling my name and then throws herself into my arms.

'Leah, I thought I told you to get yourself away from here?'

'How could I go after you chased off after Sasha and Erin?' She pulls back, studying me hard.

The blood drains from my face. I'd completely forgotten that Leah witnessed the two figures below us when we were on the chair lift. She saw me race after her sisters.

'What happened to Erin?'

Leah's not going to believe us if we say we have no idea. I'm going to have to tell her the truth.

'I've got to get Freya,' Sasha says, turning swiftly and extracting herself from the conversation.

I steer Leah away from the doors of the restaurant and we shelter under an awning along the side of the building. Running my hands through my short hair, I try to work out how to impart the news to Leah. How to make her see that everything happened in a blur. My face creases with emotion.

'She's dead, isn't she?'

'What?' I splutter, unable to see how Leah has jumped to the correct conclusion so fast.

'Erin was knocking Sasha away from the safe run, that much was clear. I looked on my maps app and the direction you were all going in... Erin was manoeuvring Sasha towards a black run. And, beyond the black run, it looked like the mountain edge was...' Leah's voice fades, the reality of what she's saying sinking in.

Still shell-shocked, I nod. I tell Leah I found them just after they'd gone over the edge. Leah's blue eyes widen in horror.

'They *both* went over the edge?' Her voice is high-pitched.

'Yes, Erin pushed Sasha. I saw it.'

I explain that Sasha managed to hold on but Erin did not. That's as close to the truth as I'm going to share. Leah doesn't need to know the upsetting minutiae.

Leah swears. 'She's really dead?'

'Well she fell... it's such a long way down. She won't have survived it.'

Leah is shaking her head and wringing her hands. 'What happens now?'

'You go, just like we planned. Get yourself as far away from this mess as possible.'

'But Jasper and Ophelia, what will happen to them?'

'I'll take care of them, don't you worry.'

'No, I can't go without seeing them. I need to at least give them a hug.'

I nod, understanding she needs to do this. Then I hurriedly run through the version of events Sasha and I are sticking to. It means we can't declare Erin is dead and we will leave it a few hours before we report her missing.

'This is... I can't believe she's gone.' Leah looks as though she's about to burst into tears. 'What a horrible way to—'

'Sssh,' I warn her as a couple of people pass us. 'Freya will be out soon. You can't say anything to anyone, promise?'

Leah nods in agreement just as Freya comes bounding towards us.

'I had the best time!' my granddaughter exclaims.

Plastering a smile on my face, I do my best to engage in small talk, asking what she did and what her favourite parts of the afternoon have been. At least she was sheltered from everything that was going on.

Leah and Sasha trudge behind me, I'm aware of them whispering together. I strain my ears to hear but I can't pick up on what they're saying. The wind is blowing too strong. As we pull up outside Snow-fall chalet, I notice that Marnie is at her window and the curtains are twitching. It dawns on me there's something about that woman that feels odd. I can't quite put my finger on it. She seems so nice, but perhaps that's the problem – she's a bit too nice.

Bracing myself, we enter the chalet. The scent of Erin's perfume hits me immediately. For a second I allow myself to believe that she's here. That, somehow, she pulled herself to safety and raced us back to the chalet. But I know that's wishful thinking. My lip wobbles as I walk into the space that she so carefully created. It's going to be hard to be here in this building, with reminders of Erin all around me. We're going to have to wait things out for a little while here, for appearances' sake, surrounded by all of Erin's things. So I'm just going to have to get through the next few days before I can take the twins and fly back to England.

'Hello gorgeous!'

Internally I groan.

'Hi,' I respond curtly.

Craig is still here. He's standing in front of me, larger than life with his leering smile and muscular figure. I hadn't taken him into account at all. The thought of sleeping under the same roof as him makes my skin crawl. I don't like the idea of him being in the same place as the children either but I can't exactly kick him out. We haven't mentioned that Erin is missing yet and, even when we do, we can't go against her wishes while she's still presumed alive. So, as if things aren't difficult enough, we're going to have to manage with Craig in the chalet as well. I just hope he doesn't get suspicious about anything.

'Nadia, don't be like that.' Craig folds his meaty arms across his chest and raises his eyebrows. It's exactly the same mannerism Erin had. And it almost undoes me.

Smoothing out my expression, I decide to change tack and at least be civil to make the next few days more tolerable.

'It's a shock seeing you, Craig. I wasn't expecting it.' I pause and then add, 'I'm going to make some dinner, would you like some?'

Craig cracks a smile. 'Do you even need to ask?'

Leah, Freya and Sasha disperse into the chalet and I set to work in the kitchen. Doing something routine, something to keep me occupied, is just what I need right now. I'm aware things are going to kick off soon and with Craig being around, he could cause problems so I need to have a plan to deal with him.

Then, just as I'm dishing out lasagna and green vegetables onto various plates, an idea comes to me.

Craig stands at the doorway to the kitchen. My skin prickles as I know he's watching my every move. I hate him being so close.

Turning to smile at him, I realise that instead of Craig being an issue, he could be the answer to our problems.

And I might finally be able to get my revenge for Simon's death.

Chapter Thirty-Three

Sasha

'Where's my mummy?' Ophelia is sitting opposite me at the dinner table and her green eyes bore into mine. She looks so much like her mother.

My fork clatters onto my plate and I pick it up again hastily. 'She went out to the slopes,' I say, trying to keep my voice normal.

Ophelia shifts in her chair, flicking her red hair over her shoulder. 'When will she be back?'

Craig's eyes dart to the window. 'There's a lot of snow coming down.'

'She probably didn't want to walk back in this weather,' Leah suggests. 'There's plenty to do at the ski village, maybe she's waiting it out there.'

Ophelia accepts this but Craig's eyes flicker towards the window once more. His presence is making me nervous. I wish he wasn't here.

I've spent the last hour in my bedroom, alternating between staring at the ceiling and sobbing into my pillow. The relief of still being here, of getting out of that situation unscathed, is overwhelming. It's also mixed with the shock of Erin coming after me and then the suddenness of losing her like that. I don't think I'll ever get over it.

Pushing broccoli around my plate, I attempt another mouthful. Eating is the last thing I want to do right now but Mum has said we need to act like nothing's happened.

'Freya, come and sit at the table,' I say firmly. She already had food as part of her ski session booking so she's not really hungry and has been hopping back and forth between the table and the sofa.

'I've had my dinner,' she whines.

'Do as your mother says,' Craig barks, his voice sharp.

Freya looks alarmed and obeys straight away. I don't want this man anywhere near my daughter, let alone ordering her about. But I can't create an argument about this now. I need to keep my head down and power through the next bit. So I keep chewing the broccoli.

My mind goes over and over Erin's final words. She told me she was in on the plan to kill Aaron and that she had an affair with Jesse. Two pieces of information that have torn apart everything I thought I knew. I wonder if she felt like this when she was lying, if she felt tense and afraid. Or if she was relishing every part of it.

The dinner is painful and agonising. I swallow bite after bite until my plate is empty, and I'm forced to listen to Craig going on about his plans for the future. How he can't wait to do this and that. Then he and Jasper get onto the subject of football and, thankfully, I can tune out that conversation.

'The weather's not getting any better,' Craig remarks, as we finish up and tidy the table. 'I might give Erin a call.'

He slopes off into the hallway. Leah glares at me. We had to let her in on what happened – Mum said she saw Erin chasing me. It's clear she doesn't feel she can leave the ski resort now. I trust Leah and at least neither she nor Mum know about my parting kick. I'll carry that knowledge to the grave with me.

With Craig out the way, I take it as an opportunity to disappear. Instead of heading back to the room I've been staying in, I slip into Erin's. As soon as I'm through the door, just seeing her belongings makes my stomach lurch with emotion. I hesitate, almost turning to leave straight away but there's something I need to know.

Opening Erin's wardrobe I scan the contents. Not finding what I'm looking for, I rapidly open the drawers to her bedside table and then work through her dressing table. I slide the bottom drawer open and discover Erin's laptop.

Flipping it open, I realise finding it was the easy bit. Next, I need to break through her password. I enter a few options, variations of the twins' names and Erin's properties, but to no avail. Just when I think my search is going to prove fruitless I hear a dinging noise. It's not the laptop, it's something else in the dressing table drawer. I crouch back down and see Erin's iPad. Snatching it up, I swipe it open. I know the four-number password to this because I heard Jasper saying it the other day.

Tapping into the screen, I survey the different icons and swiftly select mail. I need to see for myself if there was any email communication between Jesse and Erin. I know I'm torturing myself by doing this, but I need to know why. Why it happened and when it started. Jesse isn't going to tell me the truth and Erin's gone now. I need more details in order to make sense of it all.

Scrolling through the organised mailbox, I can see there are only a handful of messages to my husband's email address. And none are written communication between the two of them, all of the messages are hotel bookings that have been forwarded on. I can see half a dozen locations that they booked in the past year. I click through all of them and see each hotel was less than an hour away from the family home I shared with Jesse.

I want to fling the iPad across the room and for it to smash into tiny pieces. The sting of betrayal hurts even more now that I know Jesse wasn't just infatuated with my sister, they had a physical relationship too. Before I act on impulse, an email at the top of Erin's sent box snags my attention. It's a message to Craig Turner.

Curious, I scroll down the email chain. There are multiple messages; from Erin, the tone is very gushy whereas from Craig the correspondence consists of encouragement and coded instructions at first peppered with a frustration of being locked in his cell. Later, his elation at being released weaves into every sentence.

I read through more slowly, trying to decipher what Craig's messages are referring to. And then the penny drops. Of course. Erin was in contact with Craig, and then suddenly there was a plot to murder Aaron. Erin's confession made it sound as though it was all her idea and that she was Jesse's puppet master. But there was another layer to things; like the unravelling of a parcel, I've finally got to the surprise at the core. My biological father must have guided Erin towards taking drastic action.

The emails are cleverly worded, so that anyone without any knowledge of the crime wouldn't have a clue what they were discussing. In retrospect it all makes sense though. Erin wanted her relationship with Craig to work and she was fed up with Aaron. Craig presumably wanted to help Erin get out of her controlling relationship and get her hands on the money. So he helped in the only way he knew how.

I shudder. Craig has been responsible for so much turmoil in our family, but this really is more than I thought he was capable of. I slide the laptop back in the bottom drawer but I take the iPad back to my room. I'm going to need to show this to my mum because if Craig has been meddling this much in our family affairs from afar there's no telling what he will do now he's out of prison.

However, I only get as far as the hallway. I can hear raised voices. It's Craig and my mum.

'She's not answering her phone!' Craig thunders.

'She's a grown woman,' Mum bites back. 'You missed the teenage years when a parent has to worry about what their child is up to. She's an adult now.'

Craig growls. 'She went out to ski and look at the weather. She's not answering her phone either.'

'It's not been that long, I'm sure she'll be fine. Erin is an experienced skier.' My mum is firm but she follows up with: 'I'll ring down to the ski village and see if anyone is still out on the slopes or if she's been seen in one of the facilities if it puts your mind at ease.'

'I'll go down there,' Craig barks back.

'No, don't be ridiculous. There's no point in you going out in that weather if Erin's cosied up in a bar or at the spa or something. I'll call.'

Craig accepts this and their tense exchange comes to an abrupt halt. I retreat to my room to find Freya crashed out on my bed, sleeping soundly. So I continue looking through Erin's iPad to find out more about what she and Craig have been up to.

An hour later, the door opens and my mum and Leah join me. I show them what I've found. Within minutes, my mum has her mobile phone clamped to her ear. Her mouth set in a grim line.

We hear someone at the other end of the line speak in French; I don't understand what they're saying. I just pray they'll be able to interpret my mum's words.

She speaks slowly and clearly. 'Hello, I need to report a crime.'

Chapter Thirty-Four

Nadia

'His name is Craig Turner. And he's killed someone. I saw him do it.'

My hands are trembling as the lie trips easily off my tongue. The calm, controlled voice on the other end of the line switches to English and asks for my details and location, for me to repeat the crime I'm reporting, and if I can give any additional details. I do so without hesitation. I state that I saw Craig Turner murder Xavier Knight and take a deep breath as the person at the other end of the phone tells me to hold the line. Undoubtedly, the phone operator will be escalating this to someone more senior. All they need to do is run a check on Craig's name to find out that he's recently been released from prison after serving over thirty years for multiple murders. And then I'm certain they'll come for Craig quickly.

As I wait for the officer to get back to me, I think back over all the years I've known Craig and I curse the day I met him. Craig has done nothing but destroy this family over and over again. First when he lied to me repeatedly about his criminal activities, then an armed robbery went a step too far and he was responsible for the death of an innocent man. That left me holding one little baby and about to give birth to another on my own. Then, when I'd got my life together and I was the happiest I've ever been, Craig organised Simon's accident and death.

I've never gotten over the loss of the love of my life. And now Sasha has found proof that Craig influenced Erin's decision to bump her husband off. He prodded and poked, and suggested and aided her line of thinking. From their email exchanges, it's easy to see how eager Erin was to please her father.

The one, small comfort of finding this out is the knowledge that Erin didn't instigate Aaron's murder all on her own. She had Craig encouraging her and Jesse giving her even more of a reason to do it. What she did was still wicked, but at least a part of me can cling onto the hope that if she hadn't had either of those men circling round her, then maybe she might have chosen a different path. But the past can't be changed now and I've lost one of my daughters because of Craig. So it's time to get him out of our lives for good.

'Can you give me your location again please?' The female voice comes over the phone.

I repeat the address with specific instructions on how to find this particular chalet. 'We'll have a team of people out to you immediately. Can you let me know who else is in the property?'

Slowly, I list off the names of everyone here and I highlight that we have three children amongst us.

'Is there any way you can get the children out of the chalet?'

'Not with the weather like this.'

'You're sure Craig isn't currently armed?'

'Not as far as I'm aware.'

We end the conversation; the wheels have been set in motion now. So I've just got to pray everything turns out how I want it to.

'They're on the way,' I tell Sasha and Leah. Sasha is biting her nails and looks stressed. Leah and I have now told her about Xavier's death.

I thought Sasha was going to go to pieces but she's holding it together and Leah is calm, bracing herself for the next step.

'Craig, we're just putting the children to bed.' I round up Jasper and Ophelia, who've been watching an old western film with Craig. Both the twins groan at this.

'Five more minutes?' Jasper pleads.

'No, Freya's already asleep and you should be too.' With any luck, the children won't hear the police arriving or Craig's impending arrest.

As I tuck Erin's children into their beds, I go over the story I've spun to the police. I've told them I think Craig is responsible for Xavier Knight's murder. Craig arrived hours before Xavier's death, so he was at the ski resort when Xavier met his end. Part of my reason for accusing Craig is that I want to make sure Erin's name isn't dragged through the mud. Leah has deleted the voicemail message of Xavier calling out Erin's name, and I'm sure that's not enough evidence for the police to believe Erin was responsible. Erin's phone has tumbled into the ether with her but there's no telling where Xavier's device might be and the police will be scrutinising it. I also want to protect Leah because she was one of the last people to see Xavier alive. There's no doubt the police will be questioning us all but if we stick to our stories and say Craig is responsible then there's a chance they might leave us alone.

I strain my ears but I can't hear any sirens or the sounds of approaching cars outside. Pointing the finger of blame in Craig's direction has the added bonus of giving him a whole world of hassle. Things are about to get very hot under the collar for my ex-husband. And when the time comes to report Erin as a missing person, I'll be sure to pretend to the police that Craig has something to do with that as well.

The truth is, Craig isn't responsible for either Xavier's death, or Erin's disappearance, but there are plenty of other things he's gotten away with and I want him back in prison, away from my family. This is the perfect route to achieving that.

I also want the heat off me.

Because there's something that neither Sasha or Leah knows.

Craig definitely didn't kill Xavier. But I'm also certain that, despite how things seem, Erin didn't murder him either. How do I know that?

Because I did it.

I watched Xavier etching a creepy message in the snow the first night we were here. At first I thought it was meant for Leah but then I overheard Xavier threatening Erin. On the night he died, Xavier came to Snowfall Chalet a few hours into his evening with Leah. He told Erin he needed to speak with her privately outside. I watched their exchange from my bedroom window. Erin was visibly shaken and asked where Leah was; he told her not to worry because Leah was still back at his chalet. But he hinted that he wasn't above using Leah as a pawn in his game.

Xavier was blackmailing Erin, telling her that he saw her involvement in Aaron's death and that he would reveal her secret to everyone and ruin her life. He wanted money – of course. By the sounds of things he'd blown a pretty hefty inheritance left by his grandfather in a very short amount of time and he wanted an investment in Burcott House. He could see how lucrative it was and he wanted to be part of that. Xavier made the mistake of thinking Erin would be vulnerable without Aaron. She gave him as good as she got and told him in no uncertain terms that he wouldn't be getting a penny from her. But he wasn't about to give up and I was afraid Erin might end up being arrested if Xavier did decide to make trouble for her.

So, after Xavier finally left, I followed him back to his own chalet. As I watched in the shadows, I could make out there had been some sort of party and there were still a few stragglers smoking on the porch. I could see some activity through the window as well. I almost turned back. It wasn't the ideal circumstances to carry out my intentions. But I knew if I didn't act now then I might lose my nerve and not go through with it. Or Xavier might follow through on his threats to expose Erin's involvement in Aaron's death. And then everything I had done to protect Erin would've been for nothing.

I didn't have a plan but I'd wrapped up well and made sure to put on more layers than usual in case I was outside for a while but, even with all the material my body was swathed in, I was still getting cold fast. And then someone dropped a lit cigarette on the porch. I was near enough to hear them stamp it out and the ensuing argument between the two people standing together. One sentence floated towards me:

'Whoa! Watch it! This place could go up in flames.'

That gave me an idea. Brazenly, I approached the chalet. My hood was still up and I just had to cross my fingers that no one tried to talk to me. I calculated there were ten or twelve other people milling around the chalet, including Xavier who was inside. So I casually entered through the door and swiped a bottle of something that had been discarded on the kitchen worktop to help me blend in. I watched as Xavier went off to the bathroom – it was perfect timing. I jammed a chair up against the handle to stop him from getting out.

It didn't take me long to locate the second thing I was looking for: the fire alarm. It was tucked away in the hallway, just out of sight of the main room. I'm not the tallest person but the combination of dragging a large plant pot to stand on and using the bottle in my hand meant that I could jam the fire alarm button in such a way that it got stuck.

The sound of the alarm blared out across the party. I hastily shoved the plant pot back into position and then made my way back into the central room of the chalet to usher people out.

'Party's over!' I called.

Everyone was in such a scramble to get out, no one even glanced in my direction. My plan was working. And there was only one thing left to do.

Xavier banged to try and get out of the bathroom but gave up once the fire alarm stopped squawking. I listened to him pacing around inside and calling out 'Erin!' – he must have heard me outside the room and jumped to the conclusion that Erin was behind the jammed door. I then heard a muffled conversation and cursed under my breath. At the time, I had no idea who he was trying to call and I was worried that someone might turn up to aid his escape from the bathroom. But now I know this was when Xavier contacted Leah and left a voicemail message for her, telling her all about Erin's involvement in Aaron's death. Another fifteen minutes went past and then his movements stopped. Gently, I prised open the door and found Xavier passed out on the bathmat. At that point I hesitated: I wasn't sure if I could go through with it. Then I thought of Erin losing her freedom and I knew it was the only answer.

Xavier was in a deep sleep; he wouldn't have been aware of me covering his mouth and nose. His ending was quick and clean – or so I thought. It was when I was hefting him out into the living room to carry out the next stage of my plan that he started twitching. I panicked – and then I saw the kitchen knife. I used it. Xavier was a tall, strapping man and I was scared he might come round and overpower me. But I'm a strong, physically fit woman. I'm used to lifting weights in the gym and because Xavier was groggy I had the upper hand. It wasn't meant to be so violent but that's how Xavier's life eventually ended.

My plan had been to set the chalet alight and burn it down, along with the evidence. But I got spooked. I thought I heard a noise outside the chalet and I went to investigate. Once I had stepped away from Xavier, I couldn't go back. I couldn't look at what I'd done. So I fled the chalet, leaving the knife and the body behind. I managed to get rid of my gloves and my clothing by dumping them in a communal bin before anyone noticed the blood-splattered garments.

I'm not proud of my actions. I know it makes me just as bad as Craig. Except the difference is, I did what I had to in order to protect my daughter. I would've done anything for Erin, even though she'd got herself into such a mess. However flawed Erin was, she was still my child. I carried her inside me for nine months – that's a bond you cannot break. Still, it makes my skin itch just thinking about what I did to stop any questions being asked about Erin's part in Aaron's death. Xavier was a fool to think he could bully my Erin – and he was a fool to think he would be able to manipulate her to his advantage so easily. He underestimated the Bailey women.

'If we stick to our story, it will all be fine,' I say to reassure Sasha and Leah as well as myself. Then I hear a car outside, driving along the gritted road.

'It must be them!' I jump up faster than my body is used to and peek out of the window. There's a sleek, grey car directly in front of the chalet. The sirens aren't on, but perhaps that's because they want the advantage of surprise.

Anticipation bubbles up inside me. This is it. This is the moment Craig is carried back to a cell and out of my life for good. And I can't wait to see the back of him.

I hear the pounding on the blue door of the chalet and then the unmistakable noise of people breaking into the property. I wait for Craig's shout of surprise.

But it doesn't come.

Instead, I hear the French police shouting for Craig, bursting into each room but with none of the expected responses from the person they're hunting down. My heart drops and I have a feeling in my soul that something has gone wrong.

Striding into the hallway, I join the search while explaining to the police who I am. Soon it's clear that Craig has vanished.

'Where is he?' I cry in frustration.

Sasha joins me, worry chiselled across her features. It's no use. He's no longer under this roof.

There are five members of the French police here. One is reporting back, barking short responses into a crackling walkie-talkie, another is continuing to search behind every curtain and in each corner while the other three mill about. I catch one of them eyeballing me suspiciously.

Dashing to the open door, I stand shivering under the porch of the chalet. Looking up and down the long stretch of empty pathway, I wonder where Craig is. Why did he do a runner? Did he get an inkling of what was about to happen? And, if so, how?

There's a movement across the way and it startles me. I see Marnie standing at her bedroom window, she's looking down at the unmarked police vehicle outside Snowfall Chalet and then she glances up and sees me staring at her. Her brows are knitted together and her posture is rigid and stiff.

I'm musing as to whether she might have seen which way Craig escaped but she pulls her curtains very tightly shut before I can signal to her. I'll ask the police to speak to her to check if she saw anything.

I go back indoors to my daughters. Sasha and Leah look expectantly up at me. I shake my head slowly.

'He got away.'

Sasha and Leah's faces mirror each other. They both look petrified.

This isn't good news for our family, especially if Craig suspects that one of us is responsible for calling the police. And now I'll have to sit down and go through question after question with the authorities, explaining why I believe he's involved in Xavier's death and Erin's disappearance.

I thought my plan would work and that everything would come full circle. With Craig back behind bars, I'd be free to live my life again and so would my children and grandchildren. That's still within reach, we're on a snowy alp and the weather is dire. The chances of him getting out of the ski resort tonight are slim. But I have a horrible feeling that he's going to evade the police.

A wave of panic washes through me.

If he somehow manages to get away then I'll forever be looking over my shoulder, waiting for the day he comes for me.

Chapter Thirty-Five

Sasha

I think I'm going to go crazy. We're stuck in this chalet, marooned here without any idea of when we will finally be able to leave. Everything is in limbo. It's been three days and the police still haven't found Craig. His whereabouts is currently a mystery. The sniffer dogs managed to track his scent and followed it half a mile across the resort but then lost the trail.

Police officers and undercover detectives are still teeming about outside, speaking rapidly into their walkie-talkies or shouting instructions at each other. Their activity feels frantic and yet, so far, it's not producing any results. Sighing, I unscrew the lid to my red nail polish. I've just taken off the chipped, pink colour I had on previously and the acrid smell of the nail polish remover hangs in the air around me. Trying to find things to keep us all occupied whilst we've been ordered to stay inside is starting to become overwhelming. But, for the moment, the children are playing a board game and so I'm taking the opportunity to try and focus on a task for myself.

The radio is playing in the background. Even though I don't understand the words, the tone of the beautiful French music is soothing. I try to relax my brain and concentrate on the soulful sounds and the action of the brush stroke on my nails. My shoulders begin to loosen and, for a blissful fifteen minutes, I cast away my cares. And then the music stops and the sharp voice of a young woman rings through the radio waves. The varnish on my nails is still wet so I don't want to risk smudging it by attempting to push buttons on the retro radio set to switch it off. But then I hear the name 'Craig Turner' spoken in a thick French accent and I wish I had shut the radio station off seconds before. It sounds like another news bulletin about his disappearance. If there were any updates the police would've contacted us.

I shake as the words wash over me. I don't feel safe here. Knowing that Craig is out there, possibly still somewhere close by. He might even still be in the ski resort. The police are conducting door to door searches but there are thousands of chalets here and even more people. This is one of the biggest ski resorts in France and there are multiple ways in and out.

Our chalet has been ransacked; everything has been tipped upside down in the search for any clues or evidence. His passport hasn't been discovered so he had the presence of mind to take it with him when he ran. This means that, despite my fears about him being nearby, it's more likely that he's already halfway across Europe. A red flag has been put next to his passport internationally at major airports but there are plenty of other ways that he could be travelling.

I would much rather that he was caught and sent back to jail but if that doesn't happen I just have to hope that he goes as far away from us as possible. And, if he has any sense, he'll stay away.

I blow on my fingers in an attempt to dry the nail varnish quicker before placing my splayed fingers back on the worktop. It was less than a week ago that Erin was standing in this very spot, making breakfast.

The scene on the mountainside feels like a crazy nightmare but it happened and my sister is gone.

I gulp back a sob. Erin and I were always at loggerheads, but I didn't realise she hated me quite as much as she did. Even still, I would never have wished for things to end up the way they did. The echo of her scream still rings in my head. I'll never forget it.

When the police first descended on us they were relentless in their questioning. Initially, they asked us a stream of queries and our responses were scribbled untidily in notebooks and captured on voice recordings. After a few hours, once Xavier's body had been located and everyone realised that Craig wasn't going to be captured easily, we were carted off to the police station for more intense interrogation. Me, Leah and mum were all in there for hours. I was absolutely terrified. We were told that we were just there to help with the investigations but I didn't like the manner in which we were being treated. It was evident the authorities mistrusted us. It was like reliving the conversations with the English police in the wake of Jesse's arrest all over again.

And then when Erin didn't materialise, questions started being asked about her. The three of us told the police that she'd gone skiing just before Craig fled the chalet. It was the only information we shared. So, after forty-eight hours, Erin was officially declared a missing person. Staff at the ski resort have been out looking for her on the mountain tops since the moment her absence was highlighted. The police are currently treating her disappearance as in connection with Craig's. They suspect Craig has either taken Erin with him or killed her. I dread the time when they do discover her frozen body and the questions that might be asked.

Tapping each nail, I make sure that the varnish has dried before going to fill a glass of cold water. Lately, I've been reaching for the drinks cabinet way too much. But in the last few days I've not touched a drop. The shock of Erin's fall along with the police presence has given me the reality check I needed. It's up to me to stop myself spiralling into alcoholism. On that mountain edge, fearing for my life, I vowed that if I made it back to Freya then I'd start afresh. And that's what I'm doing. Staring death in the face has made me realise that I want to make the most of my life. I almost hit rock bottom and now the only way is up. I know the next few months are going to be difficult, and many more challenges will be sent my way, but I'm ready to face them.

As soon as we get out of here, I'm going to find somewhere for me and Freya to start again – and mum and Leah too if they want to join us. The past is painful, but I'm not going to let it ruin my future.

The doorbell rings loudly – once, twice, three times in quick succession. I straighten up, smooth down my hair and yank open the door.

It's the police.

I brace myself for whatever is about to come next.

Chapter Thirty-Six

Craig

The game is up; they've found me.

The sirens scream and the sound of several boots pounding the pavement come towards me as I turn down an empty side-street. I managed to hide out in an unoccupied chalet for the last few days but now I'm back out in the cold and running from the law again. I feel breathless as I try to keep the distance between me and those trying to bring me down. The chances of me losing them are slim, but I'm not going to give up without a fight.

For the last few days, I've lucked out because the chalet I gained entry to was quite something. It was even bigger than Erin's and there were silk sheets on the bed, fancy soap in the shower and even packets of food in the cupboards. It wasn't a bad way to be holed up – I've been in much worse situations. Kicking back with a can of drink I haven't had to pay for and watching whatever I wanted on TV was a decent way to pass the time. I thought the local police might get fed up looking for me.

With the snow falling so heavily, the sniffer dogs were no use. I watched them from the bedroom window, scouting around the chalets a couple of roads away. They hadn't got a clue. But I was also trapped here until the extreme weather warnings blaring on the news calmed down. My options for escape were limited – I didn't fancy trekking across the Alps to find freedom. Julie Andrews I am not. So I was using the last few days to plot my escape – but unfortunately the police have got to me first.

Along with the weather warnings, the news dominating the local area was the death of a posh bloke called Xavier Knight. From what I've gathered, Nadia has pointed the finger of blame for his death at me. I didn't think she hated me that much. But the other news story that has been even more worrying is the disappearance of a thirty-something millionaire on the mountaintops. My Erin.

Her beautiful face has been flashing up on every news report. There are search parties out there for her. They've come across a set of abandoned skis, a pair hired from the resort, which tallies with her last movements. So the outlook isn't positive. I've been glued to the updates because I really do care for her. I've also got a feeling in my old bones that she's not dead. She's the sort of person who can get themselves out of trouble, however bad it is. They haven't found a body and, until they do, I will continue to believe that she's out there somewhere.

I wanted to go and look for her myself. But I've got a target on my back. I'm fuming that Nadia's fitted me up for a murder and I'm even more angry that she's also accused me of being behind Erin's disappearance as well. I know this because Erin's helpful neighbour, Marnie, has been keeping me updated on my burner phone. Of course they were going to look in my direction first and because I've run, not wanting to risk interrogation and more years behind bars, it's made me seem more guilty. Even though this time I'm innocent.

I don't know who killed Xavier but it wasn't me. I didn't do it. I can't help thinking this is something to do with Erin. She may have got a taste for murder. Then again, I think she would've told me what she was up to. Especially if things hadn't gone to plan. So that's made me suspect someone else is behind it. One thing is for sure, the Bailey women all have secrets and I'm in the dark. It could've been any one of them.

If the owner of the chalet hadn't turned up this morning, I might have managed to get away after a few more days. My plan was to try and sneak onto the train out of the resort once the police presence had fallen away. But they're on top of me now and there's no way I'm getting out of this.

It was good of that Marnie woman to warn me the police were outside in the first place. At least that gave me a bit of time to attempt an escape, even if I've ultimately failed. I know Marnie and Erin were close, and the woman did me a good turn.

Nadia has done well to get the police and media on her side. I didn't think she had it in her, but she's pinned the blame on me. She even did a news appeal for Erin – complete with crocodile tears – asking for the public to look out for me too. She's told everyone that she saw me kill a man who I've never even met. I'm furious that resources are potentially being diverted away from the search for my daughter just because my ex wants me back in a cell.

They're closing in on me now. As I glance over my shoulder, a burly officer is just an arm span away from me. My feet falter as his hand clamps on my shoulder. I know I'm about to hear the words I've dreaded: 'You're under arrest…'

But I don't care what happens to me next. I've spent most of my life in prison. My fate was influenced by my father, my family and the web of crime I grew up in. It dawns on me as I face the sweating officer who's about to put my hands back in cuffs that spending my final years as a free man was just a dream. I probably wouldn't have lasted very long on the outside any way.

The only thing I have left to hope for now is that Erin is alive.

Chapter Thirty-Seven

Leah

Erin's body hasn't been found. It's been a week and the authorities haven't been able to retrieve it. They've said in cases like this, when someone goes missing in these Alps, even in such close proximity to a well-used ski resort, it can take years for the body to be found. And sometimes it never turns up.

I couldn't leave my family, not after what Sasha went through with Erin. And Mom is broken by the loss of her middle daughter. So I stayed. We've made the decision to fly back to England together. After an intense period of interviews with the police – about Craig, Xavier and Erin – they're satisfied enough with our answers that we've been allowed to leave the country. Mom was convincing in her argument that Craig was responsible for Xavier's murder and Erin's disappearance. Even I nearly believed her. The French police have taken the way Craig bolted as a sign of guilt. They also discovered that Marnie had warned Craig the police were on to him. Unfortunately for her, there's evidence in the form of text messages so she was arrested for perverting the course of justice by trying to help him to evade the police. We were all stunned to find out that Marnie even knew Craig. I bet she's wishing she'd never got involved now.

There may not be any concrete evidence to link Craig to the crime of killing Xavier but our mom is prepared to testify to say she witnessed him end Xavier's life. It will be her word against his. We will have to wait for the judge and jury to decide Craig's fate. Hopefully it will be enough to put him permanently behind bars again but, in many ways, I wish Mom would drop the whole thing. But I understand her drive to send him back to prison. She will never feel safe if he's out in the world and there's no doubt he's a dangerous man. At least he's in custody awaiting trial at the moment.

Leaning back in the seat of the plane, I fix my gaze out of the window as the aircraft rolls down the runway and then takes off. My stomach lurches as we soar into the sky. Thinking of Xavier hurts. I thought we were at the start of something special. Now, I will never know. The loss of someone so young, only just starting to live their life, has rocked me. It's really brought it home that, whatever age you are, you just don't know what's around the corner. I still don't know who killed Xavier. It may have been Erin; I'll never know the truth. But, as I've discovered that sometimes it's best not to.

Scanning the cabin, looking at the sea of tourists seated around me, I can see many of them are also travelling back from a winter break but I bet none of them have had an experience quite like mine. At least Craig has now been caught. And, with any luck, he'll be back behind bars in no time.

Erin's loss has ripped through our family. Jasper and Ophelia have been devastated. I think they're both still holding onto the hope that she might be found. Mom said there was no way Erin would have been able to survive that drop, but for the children this period of time might mean they get used to the idea of her being absent before her death is confirmed. My heart twangs with sadness for the twins. They've lost their mother and their father in a couple of short months. That's why I'm going to stay in England.

I've decided my travelling days are over, especially after the recent troubles with Lindsay and Shane. They've left me alone for the past week, but it's still on my mind. I need to sort out the mess once and for all. Now my manager and my mom know, I've got people on my side who can help. I'm going to get an injunction as a starting point and then try to salvage my reputation.

Most of all, I want to strengthen my family ties. Throughout this rollercoaster few months, that's what's hit home for me. No matter how crazy they might all be, family is the most important thing. It's already been decided that Jasper and Ophelia will live with Aaron's father and stepmother, who have assured Mom and the rest of us that we can see them regularly. I want Jasper and Ophelia to know that I'm always here for them, no matter what. I'm also planning to spend a lot more time with Freya too. I want this next phase to be different for our family.

Ophelia and Freya are sitting side by side; their hands have been clasped together for take-off. It's sweet seeing them together. Freya has been very thoughtful to both of her cousins this past week. All three of them have experienced great loss, but maybe it'll tighten their bonds and make the next generation of this family stronger.

I'm comforted a little by this thought. A smile passes between Freya and Ophelia as the aeroplane levels in the sky. I'm hoping things will become calmer once we've returned to England and that we can all help each other to re-build our lives.

But just before I close my eyes, preparing to drift off while I'm on the flight, I see something I wish I hadn't. The minute Freya looks away from her cousin, distracted by the food trolley rattling along the narrow aisle, the expression on Ophelia's face dramatically changes. Gone is the soft smile and in its place is an expression of pure hatred. Ophelia's eyes are narrowed and her lips pinched. The minute Freya turns back to face her, Ophelia relaxes her features, so her brow is once more smooth and her lips are smiling.

It happened so quickly that I could've blinked and missed it. But the flicker of emotion on Ophelia's face was there. I'm going to have to keep an eye on the pair of them.

Because we've had enough rivalries and secrets bubbling under the surface of this family to last a lifetime.

And I don't want history repeating itself.

Epilogue
Three Months Later

Chapter Thirty-Eight

Sasha

'Breaking news: the bodies of a man and a woman have been found on the outskirts of a ski resort in France. The couple's frozen remains were well preserved in the icy conditions and experts were quickly able to identify them as Australian couple Shane and Lindsay Robertson.'

My whole body trembles as I watch the news presenter on the screen in front of me share this information in such a matter-of-fact way.

'The married couple were uncovered during the ongoing search for missing mother Erin Bailey-Scott who disappeared from the resort three months ago and is yet to be found.'

I grab the remote and switch off the TV. I can't stand to listen to the details. The media are still fixated on Erin's disappearance. I get why – it's a juicy story and Erin's image is very promotable. Added to that, Erin's father Craig Turner is a known killer and is in the process of being prosecuted for Xavier's murder, plus her wealthy husband's death was well documented in the media last Christmas. There have been countless stories about Erin and someone has even set up a true crime podcast. It's relentless. And that's why the whole family – including the twins – have uprooted. We had to get away from the British press. We're currently living in a rental house in Iceland, which is supposed to be the safest country in the world.

I'm sickened to hear of the deaths of Shane and Lindsay. They might not have been very nice people, but they didn't deserve to die like that. The discovery of their bodies is another piece in the puzzle of those chaotic days at the ski resort. Leah has now told me all about the full extent of Shane and Lindsay's blackmailing. But since we left the ski resort they haven't bothered her and now we know why.

Still shaking all over, Erin's words come back to me. '*Aaron isn't the only person I've murdered.*'

Is this what she meant? Did she bump the two of them off because of the way they were harassing Leah? Or perhaps they had some sort of genuine skiing accident? As I turn the events over in my mind, it's clear to me that Lindsay and Shane having an accident would've been too much of a coincidence. I can feel it in my bones that Erin was responsible.

I'm sure the French police will discover the couple's connection to Leah and be questioning us all once more. But that's not the thing that bothers me the most. If Leah wasn't involved in their deaths – which I don't believe she was – then she should be fine. The thing that keeps me lying awake at night is the fear that Erin still hasn't been found. The police liaison officer explained to us on the first day we reported her missing that some bodies are never recovered from the Alps.

I know they've searched the area where Erin fell so it unnerves me that they didn't find her body. The bad weather may be the explanation, the heavy snowfall could've covered her up to the extent that the mountain rescue team and police sniffer dogs missed it. I'm not so sure though. The thing that's niggling at me is the knowledge there were lots of jutting ledges on that side of the mountain. Thank God, because that's what saved me. Perhaps Erin didn't fall all the way to the bottom though, maybe she disappeared from our sight but cheated death for a second time...

These are the thoughts that taunt me daily. I try to keep myself calm because it's likely Erin would've been injured by falling further and it would've been difficult for her to find her way to safety – difficult but not impossible. They're continuing the search though, so there's still a chance they will find her remains.

Until the day we get that closure, I'll always be wondering if Erin is still alive. And if I'll ever be safe...

Extract: Her Daughter's Lies

Everyone tells me I look like my mother. They say I'm the spitting image of her, with my long copper-coloured hair and bright green eyes. Apparently, I even sound like her. I know for some people that's difficult.

It's funny they never mention my father though – or speak about what happened to him. No one ever acknowledges his existence or the way he died.

Being orphaned at the age of nine was tough, but it taught me to be tough as well. It's shaped every element of my life – of course it has. But now, on the eve of my eighteenth birthday, I'm ready for adulthood. Ready for my family to stop treating me like a child. And ready to create my own life.

The first thing I'm going to do is find out the truth. I want to know what really happened to my parents.

And then I'm going to get my revenge.

You can find out what happens next to the Bailey family in *Her Daughter's Lies*. **Available to pre-order now!**

The Christmas Holiday

The perfect vacation... or the perfect murder...

Alicia Silver is spending her first Christmas holiday with her handsome new husband **Jack** and his family in their remote, luxurious lodge in the snowy Irish mountains.

The Silver family are wealthy and beautiful, and Alicia is determined to live up to their high expectations for her marriage. But with the festivities in full swing, Alicia quickly discovers that behind their perfect image, her new in-laws are hiding plenty of secrets...

The gorgeous husband
The jealous sister-in-law

The glamorous step-mother
The controlling father-in-law

Before the vacation is over one of them will be dead.

Who would kill to protect their shocking secret? And will Alicia survive this Christmas holiday?

This completely addictive psychological thriller is packed with chilling twists that will keep you up all night. Perfect for fans of Lucy Foley, Lisa Jewell and Ruth Ware.

The Christmas Holiday **is available to read now!**

Extract: The Christmas Party

Prologue

I spin with my sister in the middle of the dance floor, our hands clasped tight, whirling round to the music just as we did when we were children. The DJ is playing yet another classic Christmas tune and we both shout along at the tops of our voices, smiles wide, eyes bright, mirroring each other. Rainbow-coloured disco lights shine across the vast room and the crowd around us shimmers and sparkles.

The moment I've been hoping for is finally here. After ten long years, my family are together under the same roof again. My two sisters, my mother, our children and our husbands. We're reunited after a decade of not speaking. But I don't want to think about the terrible night that shattered our family because I've waited for this day for a long time.

As the song ends, I stagger, wobbling on my high heels and putting a hand to my throbbing head. I feel a steadying arm loop through mine and I'm guided along the edges of the friends and family gathered here to celebrate in this exquisite hotel. The hotel that my wealthy husband and I own. We've spent the last five years remodelling the place and I've poured everything into making this building a beautiful home as well as a successful business. I've worked hard to be where I am today. I may have had a little help with my husband's money and contacts but I came from nothing. So tonight I'm proud to show off amongst my nearest and dearest. And I know I've earned every single one of the admiring looks that have come my way this evening.

Everyone else seems to be in the moment, lapping up the festive atmosphere, but I'm on edge and I can't seem to properly let my hair down, despite the champagne that's flowing. A huge Christmas tree dominates one corner of the room, while the warm gold and red colour scheme spills out across the rest of the space and throughout the multitude of plush rooms beyond. Everything looks perfect on the surface. But, right now, I need to get away from the party.

When I exit through the double doors, the noise instantly dims and I feel like I can breathe properly again. I make my way along a winding corridor, my sister's hand in mine, and then we swing open another set of double doors into the grand foyer. This is the dazzling focal point of the building, with its curved marble staircase and sweeping gallery complete with a glittering crystal chandelier.

The first thing I notice is the strange silence. The music from the party shut out by the soundproofing.

The second thing I notice is the dead body. Lying spread-eagled on the white marble floor, a pool of dark red blood surrounding the head like a halo.

I'm stunned, surely this can't be happening? But my sister inhales sharply next to me so I know I'm not imagining this.

This is not a horrible dream. It's real.

My heart is hammering in my chest and my mouth feels dry. I lift my chin and make myself look once more at the person lying on the floor. I immediately recognise the broken figure at the foot of the steep marble staircase.

And I scream...

***The Christmas Party is* available to read now!**

Extract: The Couple On Holiday

Prologue

I feel content and peaceful. A calm settles over me. I can't imagine that anything bad could ever happen, here on this beautiful island...

This summer, I'm in paradise with my new husband by my side and my life couldn't be more perfect. Light is filtering through the trees as I fling my arms wide and finish my morning yoga routine. It's a ritual I complete every day, stretching my body as the sun rises. I follow this by making a coffee and sipping the hot, sweet liquid as I go for a gentle stroll.

Each morning, I vary my walk, taking in a different scene on the private Caribbean island that's my home for the summer. Yesterday, I walked down to one of the beaches and allowed my toes to sink into the soft, inviting sand. I surveyed the clear blue sea and listened to the birds twittering in the treetops. Today, my feet take me in a completely different direction. I walk round the edges of the whitewashed villa that belongs to my family, and along the twisting path that leads to the high clifftop on the north side of the island.

I skirt along the edges of the clifftop, every so often daring myself to look at the vast drop below. As I move, the tension in my muscles loosens. I manage to cover a fair distance and I find myself nearing the section of the cliff which gives way to natural steps and leads down to an idyllic lagoon. It was the place me and my husband went to on the second night of our honeymoon, over a week ago. A smile plays across my lips as I remember our romantic evening together by the sea, under the stars.

Right now, the sky is awash with beautiful deep pinks, purples and oranges. The turquoise sea contrasts beautifully and it's like I'm looking at a painting. There's a slight breeze and I enjoy the feel of the wind rippling in my hair as I watch a small fishing boat bobbing in the water. I sigh deeply, embracing the day.

Straying to the top of the steps, I look down, wondering whether I have time to descend and take a dip in the ocean before my husband wakes up. But the thought goes straight from my mind as I gaze down the steep, stony staircase and see a red trail of blood.

I freeze, panicked by the sight. It's not just a few blood spots, there's a lot of dark, red blood.

Perhaps an animal has been hurt? Or maybe someone is in trouble?

I take a deep breath, not really wanting to look again but knowing I'd never forgive myself for turning away if I could help in some way.

I stand on the first step and look down at the dizzying drop below. My nails are digging hard into the palms of my hands. I can't see anything, so I take another step, and then another until I'm part way down the route to the lagoon.

And then I see it.

I see the body, crumpled at the foot of the steps. The neck at an unnatural angle.

No-one could survive a fall like that.

I turn around, wanting to put some distance between me and the dead person, knowing I need to report what I've seen straight away. Instead, I'm jolted by the figure now standing on the top step looking down at me.

My heart hammers in my chest and I fight to keep my balance and stay upright.

Am I next?

The Couple on Holiday is available to read now!

Dear reader,

Thank you for reading *The Family Secret*. I hope you enjoyed this book. If you did, I'd be hugely grateful if you could post your review on Amazon. Reviews on Amazon make such a difference, especially for independent authors like me, and they help other readers to discover new stories too.

Leave a review!

If you were entertained and would like to find out about my new releases, you can sign up to my mailing list via the following link:: https://subscribepage.io/MikaylaDavidsBooks

Subscribe!

I love hearing from readers and your feedback is invaluable. I'm keen to hear which characters you loved to hate, the chapters that kept you most gripped and what your reactions to the twists were.

To get in touch with me, you can do so via the links below.

All my thanks,

Mikayla Davids

Follow me on Twitter: @MikaylaDBooks

Follow me on Instagram: mikayladavidsbooks

Find me on Facebook: Mikayla Davids Books

Visit my website:

https://mikayladavids.wixsite.com/mikayladavidsbooks

Acknowledgements

I've released four novels in quick succession and a lot of friends and family have helped me achieve my dream of becoming a published author. So I'm going to say 'ditto' to the cluster of wonderful people I've mentioned in my previous acknowledgements – you all know who you are! My utmost thanks to you all again, I'm so grateful for your support.

In these acknowledgements, I want to say a BIG thanks to the readers in the book community who have helped me along the way in my journey in the last year. It's been great to make new bookish friends! And I'm particularly indebted to the bloggers who've supported each book release and shared reviews far and wide – you are all amazing!

Special thanks to my VIP reader group and to Love Books Tours!

Also by Mikayla Davids

Also By Mikayla Davids

The Christmas Holiday: A totally gripping and addictive psychological thriller

The Christmas Party: An absolutely addictive psychological thriller with a jaw dropping twist (The Bailey family psychological thrillers Book 1)

The Family Secret: A completely gripping psychological thriller full of incredible twists (The Bailey family psychological thrillers Book 2)

The Couple on Holiday: A completely addictive and gripping psychological thriller with a heart-stopping twist

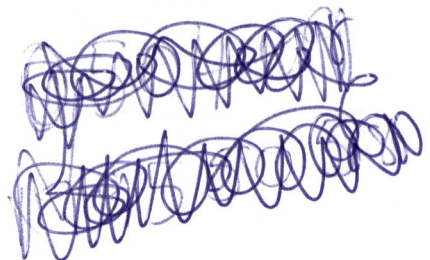

Printed in Dunstable, United Kingdom